PANHANDLE SHOWDOWN

Crime had the Texas Panhandle in a tight, bloody grip when the big stranger rode into small town of Spit Junction. By the next morning Kid Buttercup was in jail for his part in a wild saloon brawl and the local bank had been robbed. Who had killed the bank's president and left him locked in the empty vault? There were suspects a-plenty, but very little evidence. This was the puzzle to be solved by the drifting stranger turned reluctant deputy, Kid Buttercup. Tensions mounted in Spit Junction until they finally exploded in a violent Panhandle showdown.

PANHANDLE SHOWDOWN

PANHANDLE SHOWDOWN

by

Link Hullar

Dales Large Print Books
Long Preston, North Yorkshire,
BD23 4ND, England.

British Library Cataloguing in Publication Data.

BOLTON LIBRARIES

Hullar, Link
    Panhandle showdown.

    141 8756

    A catalogue record of this book is
    available from the British Library MAG   19:04:11

    ISBN   978-1-84262-773-0 pbk   F   £11:99

First published in Great Britain in 1996 by Robert Hale Limited

Copyright © Link Hullar 1996

Cover illustration © Michael Thomas

The right of Link Hullar to be identified as the author of this
work has been asserted by him in accordance with the
Copyright, Designs and Patents Act, 1988

Published in Large Print 2011 by arrangement with
Link Hullar, care of David Whitehead

Dales Large Print is an imprint of Library Magna Books Ltd.

Printed and bound in Great Britain by
T.J. (International) Ltd., Cornwall, PL28 8RW

For Sharon, Lauren and Lane with love
and for
David and Janet Whitehead with
appreciation for their friendship and
invaluable assistance

ONE

'Methuselah's ghost!' exclaimed the man sitting astride the large, dusty, roan mare. 'What a pitiful little town we done found us, Petunia!'

Petunia's ears twitched as the big man spoke. She did not resemble a petunia in any way, shape or form. One large ear appeared to have been chewed by a stray bullet, while her stringy tail and mane would have been more at home upon the end of a well-worn mop. *Ugly* described the beast more appropriately, but the mare had been called 'Petunia' for many hard years on the trail, and so 'Petunia' she would remain. The homely roan nibbled at stray brush as the rider shifted in the patched saddle so that he could look out across the arid plains toward the small collection of buildings some few hundred yards distance down the rocky road he now travelled. The flat, open spaces gave him a clear view.

'Ain't much, but it'll have to do, darlin',' he opined and, touching heels to the mare, he started forward at a slow, deliberate pace. Sage and yucca spread across the landscape. Fall had brought a cooling of the harsh summer heat, pleasant temperatures to be enjoyed before the onset of the freezing Panhandle winter. 'We'll see if we can pick up a few dollars 'round here, you beeyootee-full hunk'a horse-flesh.'

Quite simply, the man was huge. Standing six and a half feet in height and weighing in at 245 pounds, there were few who rivalled the rider in his size and build. Broad shoulders and big bones made the giant appear indestructible. The large frame was encased in dirty buckskins decorated with a rawhide fringe and sparse Indian bead-work. His scuffed knee-high boots were jammed into battered stirrups. A high-peaked, bat-tered tan Stetson was pulled down over thick, dark hair flecked lightly with grey, while a bushy moustache hid his mouth and scrubby salt and pepper whiskers stubbled his heavy, square jaw. Large-knuckled hands held the reins loosely. Deep brown eyes looked out from a knocked-around face, and they were never still. Dominating the lined, leathery face was a misshapen mass that lay in the approximate center and must once have been a quite prominent nose. At present, the twisted feature appeared unsure what direction it might take as it had been contorted by numerous breaks over many long years of a brawling life on the western frontier.

'Spit Junction, Texas,' rumbled the man as he passed the weathered sign. Without thinking his hand drifted to the weapons at his belt. The big Bowie blade hung securely at his right hip while the Remington Frontier .44 sat comfortably upon his left with the grip turned out for a rapid cross-draw. A Winchester saddle gun was sheathed within easy reach as well. Brown eyes searched the street, windows, and doorways. 'A fine howdy-do,' he grumbled, remarking upon the lack of activity on this bright Friday afternoon.

The fall weather had quickly turned brisk, windy and cool. While the Panhandle folks enjoyed the change in temperatures, they stayed out of the dusty, blowing wind as much as possible. No one walked the streets as the rider entered the far end of Main Street. He surveyed the grey, wind-swept buildings with little enthusiasm. The wide path that served as the principal road through the little town was crossed by two smaller trails. Along these rocky streets stood some two dozen residences and almost as many commercial structures. Three saloons, a bank, a two-storey hotel, a livery stable, a general mercantile, a marshal's office, a doctor's surgery, a small café, a combination hardware store and gunsmith shop and a scattering of other establishments fell under the rider's scrutiny. These seemed to make up the bulk of the business district in the fading little town. All the wood evidenced the worn look that came from being baked in the Texas summer sun and then scrubbed by the freezing north winds that blew down on the high plains throughout the winter months. Spit Junction was not much to look at, but for the moment it was the only town the big man could find, so it would have to do.

'I'm lookin' fer some booze and cards,' the giant announced in a deep, booming voice as he stepped down from the saddle before the livery stable. Flipping a coin to the young man who emerged from the shadowed interior of the barn, he asked, 'Jist where in the blue blazes does a feller find sich goin's on in this here town?'

'Well, sir,' the ragged youth replied, 'the biggest and newest is the Silver Slipper. They opened up little more'n a year ago and they's got gamblin', liquor, and purty women aplenty.'

'Music to my ears, son.' A wide grin animated the man's scruffy features, exposing a few missing teeth in the otherwise even rows of ivory. 'You take good care of Petunia, boy. She's a sure 'nuff jewel.'

'Yes, sir,' the stablehand shouted as the buckskin-clad figure went stomping off in a dusty cloud. The young man scratched his head while staring at the ugly old mare in bewilderment. 'A jewel? This knobhead?'

The big man was already making directly for the bright red batwing doors and the flashy, bright red and yellow painted sign that announced the location of the Silver Slipper Saloon.

'The only fresh paint in town,' mumbled the drifter in his rumbling growl of a voice. Within moments he had pushed through the swinging doors to examine Spit Junction's finest drinking and gambling establishment. Sawdust covered the plank floor and a long, polished mahogany bar ran the full length of the room. The dozen tables were scattered about the open area with several lively games of chance already in progress in the late afternoon of this early fall day. Gilt, paint and polish sparkled at him from every direction. Decorations included half a dozen paintings of scantily clad women imported directly from Paris, France, and hung in strategic locations through the big, gaudy bar-room. It was exactly what the stranger had been looking for at the end of a long, dusty trail. 'Methuselah's ghost!' he bellowed in joyful relief, much like a weary traveller come home at last. 'I done found me an oasis in the desert! This here place'll do me jist fine an' dandy.' He rapidly closed the gap that separated him from the long bar, then slapped down a coin as he barked his order and licked dry lips with a scratchy tongue.

'Beer!' Once again the pink tongue slipped out from under the busy moustache that hid his mouth. 'Cold as you got it!'

A husky barkeep swept the coin from the counter and replaced it with a foamy mug of cool brew. 'It's as cold as you'll find it around here.'

The golden suds vanished in one long,

15

continuous draining before the stranger slammed the empty glass back on the counter and voiced a deep sigh of content-ment. He ran the back of a dirty hand along his mouth and grinned broadly at the slack-faced bartender.

'Whiskey!'

Coin and glass were exchanged once again, with similar results. Scratching himself beneath an armpit, the big man spoke again in that rumbling roar of a voice. 'Now, give me a bottle of that rotgut redeye poison an' point me toward a shore 'nuff card game.'

Providing the bottle along with directions to one of the gaming tables, the barkeep then turned to meet the needs of the other customers lining the long counter. Mean-while, the man in buckskins stalked across the room, aiming for one of the rear tables. His bottle and glass in hand, the newcomer radiated good cheer.

'Howdy!' His grin was wide. 'Mind if I join you fellers?'

He towered over the table as he awaited a

response. Three men sat at the table. One was a slick, well-dressed gent whose presence screamed professional gambler. The other two were simply working cowpokes in for a night on the town. One was short and stocky while the other long and lanky, but they were cut from the same cloth despite their physical differences. In unison, the cowboys nodded agreement while the sweet-smelling gambler spoke for them all.

'Join in, Mr...?'

'They call me Kid Buttercup,' the stranger announced as he reached out a soiled, calloused hand for a nearby chair. While he settled himself in his large frame, he let his eyes survey the other players.

'Buttercup?' the lanky cowboy asked with obvious amusement.

'That's my favourite flower,' the scruffy, rugged drifter explained with a grin that stretched from one ear to the other. 'I jist love flowers. Don't *you* fellers?'

Lanky scratched idly at his chin-stubble while Short and Stocky examined the newcomer's battered, leathery features and the flecks of grey in his dark hair.

'Kid?' the shorter cowhand queried.

'It's an old nickname,' Buttercup explained, his grin now threatening to split his face in two. Those at the table immediately relaxed in the presence of the hulking, friendly giant. 'Let's play cards, boys.'

One and a half bottles later, Kid Buttercup laughed loudly as he lost yet another hand. 'Ain't this a helluva game?' he asked of no one in particular. $53 in the hole, the Kid seemed totally unconcerned. While the two cowboys obviously enjoyed the stranger's boisterous good humour, the dude gambler looked on with cold eyes and hard, strained features. Two more hands passed before the gambler broke his stony silence.

'You, sir,' the tinhorn announced through thin lips, 'might even win a hand now and again if you were not such a clumsy cheater.'

All at once, a dangerous silence gripped the table where laughter had prevailed only a brief moment before. The cattle-punchers slid their chairs back to clear the line of fire, for such an accusation was invariably accompanied in fairly short order by gunblasts and cordite-stench.

The grin never left Kid Buttercup's face, however. 'They say it takes one to spot one, old pard,' he replied at last. He winked, laughed and ran a finger beneath his nose before continuing. 'Could be I've misunderstood the nature of your insinnerations, but it sounds to me like you could be suggestin' that I'm cheatin' at a friendly game o' cards.'

The gambler's eyes were flashing chips of ice. 'You *are* cheating,' he replied. 'And the game is no longer friendly.' He had been losing steadily along with the big stranger while the two cowhands were significantly ahead.

'Now, Mr Edwin…' began Lanky.

'Shut up!' the gambler hissed through tightly-clenched teeth. 'I've sat still for this long enough.'

Stocky tried to reason with the cardsharp. 'But why would–'

'I don't know,' the tinhorn cut in. 'I have no idea what he's up to. I only know he's cheatin'.'

'Well, Methuselah's ghost!' blurted the Kid.

'If you'd been winning, I'd shoot you for the cowardly cur you obviously are,' the tinhorn continued. 'As it is, I will merely content myself with–'

A large, bony fist crashed into the man's mouth, resulting in the immediate extraction of three teeth, which flew through the air to land in a pile of sawdust while blood suddenly splashed across mashed lips. The scented gambler promptly fell backward to land in a quiet heap under the table. A polished boot twitched momentarily, and then the man lay still.

'Why I never heard of sich a thang as that!' Kid Buttercup was on his feet now, as his two companions quickly rose from their chairs. The two cowpokes seized upon the opportunity to turn their entertaining Friday afternoon from a poker game to a saloon fight. The short, stocky man closed in from the left while the lanky one came at the Kid from the right. Without hesitation, Buttercup landed a boot toe-deep into Lanky's groin while gouging two fingers into Stocky's eyes. Screams of pain brought a grin of satisfaction to the giant's ears that quickly faded as a chair sailed his way from a nearby table. The big man ducked, but it was only the beginning of a wild time in the Silver Slipper Saloon.

To say the least, it was a brawl. Eleven men joined in the battle in an effort to bring the dusty stranger to his knees. Kid Buttercup whooped, hollered, laughed, growled, bit, kicked, gouged, cursed and swung huge fists about him with obvious delight. Tables and chairs were smashed to kindling. The floor was littered with the forms of men in a variety of broken poses. The Kid faced his final three opponents with a confident grin and a loud, booming laugh that made the glasses and bottles on the shelves behind the mahogany bar tremble.

'Come on, fellers,' he invited in a good-natured rumble. 'I've got my second wind and I'm rarin' to go.'

A burly, bald-headed man advanced on Kid Buttercup from the front while a chubby, squat figure circled to the big man's rear. The third stood expectantly to the side. Buttercup's big right fist smeared Baldy's nose across his face so that crimson spurted from misshapen nostrils and the man squealed in pain. Chubby leapt upon the Kid's back with a triumphant shout, but was quickly plucked off like a rag doll and sent flying into the man who waited for his run at the action. They both smashed into the wall with such force that one of the girlie paintings fell to join them in a tangled heap on the floor.

'Anybody else?' called out the stranger.

'No one else,' a new voice intoned.

Kid Buttercup scratched idly at his head then wiped a worm of blood away from his lumpy nose. The newcomer appeared to be in his early fifties and near six feet in height.

His slender frame carried powerful muscle that contrasted with the thinning grey hair and wrinkled face. While the worn range gear the man wore was unimpressive, the sheriff's model Colt .45 upon his hip obviously meant business, as did the star pinned to his shirt.

'I suppose I'm under arrest,' said Buttercup. It was not really a question, just an observation.

'You'd be right,' the man confirmed. 'Marshal Jack Crenshaw at your service.'

Jack Crenshaw's town-taming days were over, but the lawman was still plenty capable of keeping the peace in the small community of Spit Junction, Texas. It had been rumoured that he had some problems with the bottle behind him. Crenshaw had drifted into town a little less than a year ago, to become marshal soon thereafter. No one had any reason to regret the appointment, nor to question the ageing peacekeeper's performance of his duties.

'You mind if I git rid of these here?'

Buttercup indicated the weapons at his belt with a grin and a wink. 'They's a bit uncomfortable.'

'Please do,' Crenshaw replied, smiling in spite of himself. 'I'd be right happy to tote 'em over to my office for you. I suppose you're finished here?'

'Yes, sir, I believe I am.' The Kid sighed with a weary sigh as he placed the .44 and Bowie on the nearest tabletop, then added, 'Well, at least I know where I'll be spendin' the night.'

'That's a fact,' the marshal agreed as he stepped forward to pick up the pistol, knife and cartridge belt.

The two men started for the door as a figure quickly stepped from his vantage point just outside the batwings. A silver-haired man had stood silently at the doorway watching the confrontation at a distance. He stuffed a modified Colt Navy .36 into a holster at his right hip before moving quietly on down the street.

The Emerald Palace Saloon was a shabby bar-room with faded green paint spread in a thin coat over rough plank walls. A dozen scarred round tables were scattered about the room in haphazard fashion. Sawdust covered the floor. Little had been done by way of decoration, with only an occasional advertising poster breaking the monotony of washed-out emerald green. A wooden bar ran the length of the room while behind it stood the saloon's proud owner, Gerry O'Cooners.

''Tis a shame, Joshua, a shame.' The barkeep indicated the paper on the counter before him. Carrot-coloured hair topped a freckled face with the prominent broken nose. The features had *Shamrock* written across them while the six foot frame and scarred knuckles called out *prizefighter.* The saloon owner shook his head once more, then stabbed a finger at the headlines. 'Another stage hold-up just north of Amarillo. There's far too much of this skulduggery afoot these past few months, my friend.'

'That's a fact, Gerry,' his companion answered in even, measured tones. 'There's bound to be more here than meets the eye.' Across the scarred surface of the bar stood the tall, silver-haired man who had, only recently, observed the arrest of Kid Buttercup by Marshal Crenshaw. Joshua Easterly owned the town's hardware store and gunsmith shop. A fine figure of a man, Easterly was in his early sixties, but still a straight, powerful individual who stood over six feet tall and tipped the scales at more than 200 pounds. Broad shoulders narrowed to lean hips where a single old Colt Navy .36 rested in a worn holster on his right thigh. The walnut grip looked dark and smooth, the man's face rugged and clean-shaven. A straight nose and sharp sky-blue eyes dominated the weathered, but not unhandsome, features; simple clothing complimented the big man's strong appearance. A blue-checked shirt was stuffed into faded jeans which were, in turn, cuffed above serviceable cattleman's boots. 'I just wish I knew what it was all about.'

'Tis certain we'll be knowin' sooner or later,' the Irishman predicted. 'Trouble never seems to steer too far from Spit Junction.'

'Ain't that a fact,' Easterly grinned. Gerry O'Cooners was one of the few who shared the secret past of Joshua Easterly. For the hardware storeman was, in reality, the famous gunman Elijah West. Grown weary of the nomadic, dangerous life of a hired gun, West had allowed a scheme to go forward which pronounced him dead to the world. In fact, the old gunfighter thought from time to time, Elijah West *was* dead. As Joshua Easterly, he had found a new life in the town of Spit Junction on the high plains of the Texas Panhandle. A new life and a fine wife. The former schoolteacher was now Mrs Betty Easterly. Furthermore, a baby boy named Wheeler Easterly had recently been added to the family. He could ask for no more than continued peace, quiet and happiness. However, Easterly understood that sometimes peace and happiness had to be defended. If the lawless were allowed to roam free then there would be no quiet, family communities such as Spit Junction.

'I got a tellygram delivered on the stage just this mornin',' O'Cooners shifted the topic of conversation away from recent outlaw activity in the region to a new, more pleasant subject. The little town had no telegraph, so messages were wired to the nearest Western Union office and then brought on by stage. 'I'm pleased to announce that me beloved will be arrivin' on the stage in a matter of days.'

'No foolin'!' Easterly replied with wide-eyed amazement. 'The one and only?'

O'Cooners grinned with freckled features aglow. 'My own true love from the auld country will be me bride before the coming week is done.'

'Congratulations, Gerry!' the silver-haired man reached his hand across the counter to shake warmly with his friend. Many is the time he had heard the ex-fighter tell of his girlfriend back home in Ireland. He had left her behind some six years ago. Since that time, the man had saved every penny in order to pay the fare for his loving sweetheart to come to America and then on to Texas. Through all that time they had stayed in touch with weekly letters, each pledging faithful love and devotion.

'As we speak, Millicent is on a stage from St Louis,' the barkeep announced, shaking his head slowly in wonder and disbelief. 'She's over half-way to Spit Junction by now. The woman I love and left behind six years ago will soon be in me arms again, Joshua me friend.'

'I'm happy for you,' Easterly said softly, and met the gaze of the man behind the bar. 'Here's to a safe trip an' a happy marriage.' Each of them lifted his glass to drink to the older man's toast.

The safe trip notion caused Easterly's mind to shift back to their earlier conversation. The string of robberies that had taken place in the region over the past year had only increased in frequency and violence within the past few months. Banks, stage coaches, and cattle ranches were the targets of the outlaws. There had been shootings as well. Easterly had begun to think there was more to the rash of crimes than one might imagine. Marshal Crenshaw just watched the town and the former gunman was in no position to take any action in order to unravel whatever might be involved. Instead his mind turned to the big stranger recently arrested following the brawl at the Silver Slipper Saloon.

'Kid Buttercup.'

'What's that, now?' asked O'Cooners with a puzzled look.

'You ever heard of Kid Buttercup?'

'Let me think.' The barkeep scratched at the red bristles over his right ear. 'I think I once saw a big bear of a man in action down in San Antonio some time back. He wrecked a saloon down there with his bare hands an' when things got ugly, he carved his way out with a big Bowie knife before blastin' away with a .44 revolver he carried over to his left hip. Could that be your Kid Buttercup?'

'One an' the same.' Easterly rested his elbows on the bar. 'Now what do you suppose he'd want in Spit Junction?'

'Just passin' through, laddie,' O'Cooners suggested, examining his friend's curious expression. 'He's just passin' through.'

'Then again,' Easterly mused, sipping at the Tennessee whiskey that filled his shot glass, 'maybe there's somethin' to keep the big feller busy.'

The smile came to the silver-haired man's lips once more before he drained the glass and offered his companion a wink. With the help of Jack Crenshaw, there just might be something to keep that footloose drifter in town.

TWO

'The bank's been robbed!'

Easterly heard all the excited shouting from the folks littering the street out front of his hardware store and through the large window he watched the confused knot of citizens stream toward the small bank building several doors down from his own place of business.

For a moment he frowned. How *could* the bank have been robbed? He hadn't noticed any strangers in town. There'd been no sound of gunfire, no pound of hard-ridden getaway horses leaving town. Folks must've gotten it wrong.

In any case, the old shootist-turned-gunsmith directed his attention to other, more immediate matters. He made every effort to steer clear of this type of activity these days.

Whenever possible, he kept his gun safe in that well-worn holster and himself out of trouble. Obviously, no one was in immediate danger. He would let Marshall Crenshaw handle the investigation alone. After all, that's what the lawman was paid to do here.

Easterly refocused his attention upon the revolver that lay in several pieces before him. Putting all thought of the bank robbery from his mind, he tightened screws and applied oil with diligence. There was little doubt that he would learn about these recent events in due time, and at his age, he figured he could afford to wait.

'Not a penny left.'

The shouts continued to issue from the small crowd that now choked the doorway of the sturdy, brick bank building. A dozen or more townspeople milled about in anger, despair and confusion while the marshal worked inside with those selected to assist him.

'Great horny toads!' an old-timer croaked.

'Take a look at poor old Mr Philbertt!' a saloon-girl from the Silver Slipper commented in morbid fascination. 'I ain't never seen no such a-thing!'

These and similar exclamations were repeated again and again as those assembled got an occasional glimpse into the bank offices or overheard some snippet of conversation between the law officer and the men who had been allowed inside. Finally, Marshal Crenshaw emerged from the doorway with a determined look on his face.

'Move along!' he called in a voice that rang with authority. 'I mean break it up an' move along right *now!*'

Even more quickly than they had gathered, the small knot of curious onlookers dispersed to their homes and businesses. The marshal hitched up his belt and then turned toward his own destination with purposeful strides.

Within a very few moments, boots scuffed against the hard-packed earth outside Joshua Easterly's store. 'Mornin', Joshua,'

Crenshaw said as he stepped through the open doorway with shoulders slumped and a puzzled look on his leathery face.

'Coffee, Jack?' Easterly asked, nodding toward the big pot that sat upon the small iron stove near his display counter. 'You know where the extra cups are, so help yourself.'

'I could use some coffee for sure,' Crenshaw grumbled as he pulled an old tin mug from a shelf and then poured himself a scalding jolt. 'You just ain't gonna believe what happened last night, Joshua. I mean, I wouldn't believe it *myself* if I hadn't seen it with my own two eyes.'

'Try me.' The silver-haired man lifted his head so that his sky-blue eyes could lock upon the lawman's lined face. 'I've heard or seen most everythin' over the past sixty years, Jack. You can't say much that'd surprise me.'

'Don't be too dadblamed sure of that,' the starpacker replied, still shaking his head in disbelief. 'You ain't heard nothin' like this,

36

and that's a plain, honest fact.' Crenshaw scratched at the grey stubble covering his chin. 'You'll think I'm crazy, but this is the gospel truth of it...'

Easterly had returned his attention to the revolver, upon which he continued to work quietly and methodically. 'Just tell it,' he instructed.

The marshal took a sip of the thick coffee, then began his tale. 'This mornin' I was out makin' my rounds about town when I noticed that Philbertt hadn't opened up the bank yet.' He took another pull at the strong black brew. 'Well, that's mighty peculiar for Orson T Philbertt, so I walked on over to his house to find that he wasn't home. I knocked, shook and rattled his door, but I couldn't stir him. Anyway, the bank was locked up tighter'n a drum, but my gut told me there was somethin' bad wrong. To make a long story short–'

'I wish you would,' Joshua muttered testily.

'To make a long story short,' Crenshaw

went on, 'we got the door open with a crow-bar an'–'

'It was locked up from the outside, just as if Orson left it that way for the night?'

Crenshaw nodded his head. 'That's right. What's more, the damn' vault was closed an' locked as well. Other'n Philbertt, old Linus Waller is the only livin' soul in town who knows the combination of that big, iron vault, so we sent for him. He come directly to open the door, only for us to find every red cent gone and Orson Philbertt lyin' dead on the floor just inside the big iron door.'

'That's strange, all right,' Easterly allowed slowly. 'But I–'

'Hell,' interrupted the lawman. 'You ain't even heard the *strange* part yet!' Crenshaw lowered his voice to conspiratorial tones while a slight pink blush coloured his cheeks. 'Orson was dressed like a *woman*,'he whispered.

Easterly sat for a moment in stunned silence. Then he said, *'What* did you say?'

'You heard me right,' the marshal replied. 'I said that Orson T Philbertt was dressed like a woman. He was wearing a dress an' he'd been beat to death with a pistol-butt. The back of his skull was crushed in like a breakfast egg.'

Joshua slowly replaced the revolver back on the counter before him, then rose from his chair to cross over to the nearby stove. The news had shocked him, and no mistake. Removing a bottle of Tennessee whiskey from the cupboard beside the burners, he splashed a little bourbon into his cup, then filled it with hot coffee. The marshal held out his own empty cup for the hardware store man to repeat the process. In silence, Easterly returned to his seat behind the counter to sip at the steaming brew.

'It beats everythin' I've heard of in all my years at this law business,' commented the marshal. 'Other than askin' around town, I don't have a clue what this is all about. I mean just what in thunderation can you figger a thing like this here *means?*' He cleared his throat then began again. 'You know, Joshua, I was just wondering if maybe you think you could, oh see your way clear to, ah, lend me a hand with this…'

'I'm no lawman,' Easterly's sky-blue eyes took on an icy chill. ''Sides, I've got a store to run.'

'And I'm no detective,' exclaimed the starpacker. 'I've done a damn' good job here in this town, but I can't solve no crazy damn murder mystery and bank robbery such as this one! Come on now, Joshua, you just *got* to–'

'I'm a hardware-store owner.' Easterly met the marshal's gaze with cool determination. 'I fix a few guns and sell to the locals. That's all.' The big man behind the counter suspected that Jack Crenshaw knew who he was, but neither man had ever spoken of this past identity. With an effort, he paused to soften his tone. 'I'm too old to be runnin' all over the countryside chasin' outlaws and I'm too busy to be playin' detective. I've got a wife and a baby to look after, Jack. This here is *your* job.'

'All right, all right.' Crenshaw held up his hands to silence his friend. 'But the least you can do is think this business over and let me know if you get any ideas as to what this foolishness is all about. Somebody slipped into town, pulled a bank robbery, killed Orson Philbertt, and got out again without nobody around here any the wiser. There's *got* to be an answer to it all somewhere.'

'Not to mention why old Orson was wearing a dress,' Easterly added in a grim, matter-of-fact tone. 'I'd say it *does* make for an unusual mystery.'

'You'll give it some thought and pass along any ideas you get, won't you?' Crenshaw asked eagerly.

The big man grinned. 'That's a promise, Jack. In fact, I'll be stopping over by your office a little later this morning.' He shifted topics quickly. 'You still holding that big feller for bustin' up the Silver Slipper?'

'He's there,' replied the lawman. 'What do

you care about that saddlebum?'

'Just got me an idea is all.' Easterly had a thoughtful look in his clear blue eyes. 'You hold on to him until you talk with me.'

'Sure,' Crenshaw spoke, as he placed the empty cup on the counter separating him from his older friend. 'We still have to settle up over damages anyway. I imagine Ned Burdine is none too happy with that *hombre*.' The slender grey starpacker waved a casual goodbye before heading for his office. The old gunfighter spent the next several minutes deep in thought.

'He'll pay for those damages or rot in jail!'

Easterly heard the demanding voice as he approached the marshal's office less than an hour later. 'He was cheating at cards and started a brawl that destroyed valuable property!'

'I understand that, Mr Burdine,' Jack Crenshaw replied softly in a calm, steady, official voice. 'But that man back there,' he jerked a thumb toward the heavy wooden door that led to the two cells in the back of the office, 'he ain't got no money. He couldn't pay for those damages even if he *wanted* to.'

'That is no concern of mine,' saloon-keeper Burdine interrupted with contempt. 'Let him remain in that cell until he pays up to the last penny!'

'Mr Burdine...'

The silver-haired shootist stopped just outside the law office door, waiting for Ned Burdine to emerge. He did not have to wait long. Without a word, the tall, slender figure of Ned Burdine stalked from the office with an air of indignation wrapped about him like a cloak. Burdine was dressed in the height of fashion and sported a thin moustache that framed full lips. His dark hair smelled of scented oil while the face was delicately handsome. Although he appeared unarmed, Easterly knew that he carried a small, pearl–handled Smith and Wesson .32 in a shoulder-holster beneath that tailored suit coat. The elegant owner of the Silver

Slipper had never seemed to fit in with the little town of Spit Junction. He had drifted here from the gambling tables of New Orleans and never really found a place in the Texas Panhandle. He passed the older man with neither a glance nor a word of greeting.

Behind Burdine stomped his big German bouncer and bodyguard, Otto Wendt. Otto lumbered past the hardware store man with a nod of his shaven head. The German giant was seven feet of brawny, knotted muscle. Easterly had never heard him speak more than two words at any given time, but he did know one thing: Heaven help the man who got crosswise of big Otto Wendt or his employer.

'Trouble?' Easterly asked as he stepped through the doorway with a smile for the marshal seated behind his battered desk. It was typical of small town law offices through-out the south-west. There was a desk, a few straight-back chairs, a file cabinet, a half-full gun rack and a washstand complete with chipped bowl and pitcher. A locked door at the rear of the room led to a small cellblock where Kid Buttercup was presently residing in one of the town's two jail cells. 'I do believe that Mr Burdine is a bit agitated.'

Crenshaw grinned in response. 'He thinks the Kid can pay for all the broken furniture over at the Silver Slipper. Hell, Buttercup could hardly buy a decent breakfast and pay the livery bill on his horse.'

'What do you plan on doin' with him?' Easterly asked with genuine curiosity. 'You can't just turn him loose.'

'I'll hold on to him for a few days until Burdine cools down,' the marshal replied, lifting his booted feet to the desktop, then leaning back in his chair. 'I'll think of somethin' before too long.' Running his fingers through the thinning grey hair atop his head, Crenshaw moved on to the topic that dominated his thoughts. 'You got any ideas on this bank robbery and murder?'

'Nothin' I want to talk about,' the big gunman said, pulling up a chair before the old scarred desk. 'We all got our own suspicions an' scapegoats, but I'll wait an' see how this thing shakes out afore I speak up.'

'You think you could see your way clear to–'

'We've already *had* this conversation, Jack.'

'Hell, Joshua, you were practically the unofficial law in these parts before I showed up. Least you could do is lend a hand to help me clear up this mystery.'

'Unofficial is right.' Easterly nodded in agreement. 'But you're here now, and I ain't any kind of law anymore.' He raised a hand to stop the other from interrupting him. 'For the last time, I ain't no detective an' I'm too old to start actin' like one now. You know you can count on me if there's any real trouble, but you're on your own when it come to solvin' murders an' robberies. Now, let's not argue over this, Jack.'

Crenshaw heaved a heavy sigh of resignation. 'I know you're right. It's just that all the crime in these parts has got me down, Joshua. There's been hold-ups, rustlin' and killin' all around us over the past several months an' now we've had a murder an' bank robbery right here in town. I've been askin' around, you know, makin' enquiries, but so far I haven't turned up a single lead in this mess.'

'If I hear or think of anything, I'll be sure to let you know,' Easterly relented, before pausing and leaning forward in his chair. 'Meanwhile,' he added, 'I got me an idea.'

'What's that?' The marshal pulled his feet from the desktop, then sat up straight in his chair. 'I need all the ideas I can get.'

'You admit you can use some help, don't you?'

'Well, sure,' Crenshaw said with a puzzled expression. 'But you turned me down.'

'I ain't talkin' 'bout me.'

'Well, just what in thunderation *are* you talkin' about?'

'Even if you just had some help for a few days, to ask around town an' help you keep the peace while you investigated. That would make a big difference, right?'

The marshal nodded in vigorous agree-ment. 'But if not you, just who *have* you got in mind?'

'Kid Buttercup,' the old shootist replied with a wink and a grin. 'Make him a deputy.'

'A *deputy?*' Crenshaw exploded. 'He was accused of cheatin' at cards and then he busted up the Silver Slipper. He's a cheat, a brawler, and–'

'And a damn' fine hand with a gun,' Easterly completed with a secret smile. 'I know who he is. Both O'Cooners an' me have seen him in action before an' know him by reputation. He's a rough character, I won't deny that, but there's no wanted flyers out on him, I'll bet. You've checked. Anythin' on the Kid?'

'No,' the lawman responded. 'I checked him out last night. But I can't just take anybody off the street and make a deputy out of him. What would Ned Burdine say?'

'Since when do you care what Burdine says?' Easterly asked with a soft chuckle. 'Just let Burdine stew. Do you want to get to the bottom of this thing or not? Do you *really* want some help around here?'

'Sure I do, Joshua, but what makes you think that this Kid Buttercup can or will help out?'

'Call it a hunch.' The retired gunman shrugged his broad shoulders and added persuasively, 'What have you got to lose?'

Rising to his feet, the slender lawman shook his head with a smile turning up the corners of his mouth. 'Not a damn' thing, and that's a fact. The worst thing that could happen is that the Kid will skip town and that would just save the town the price of his feed and keep.'

Easterly waited while Marshal Crenshaw unlocked the cell-block door, then went to release Kid Buttercup from his cell. In a matter of moments, the starpacker emerged with Buttercup close behind.

'Sit down, Kid,' Crenshaw invited in a friendly tone as he resumed his own seat. 'Make yourself comfortable.'

'Don't mind if I do,' Kid Buttercup answered with good humour, and took a seat across from Easterly. He looked battered and bruised, but otherwise none the worse for wear following the saloon brawl. His big form settled into the chair near the hardware store man and he let his eyes wander over the older man seated near at hand. The deep-brown eyes shone brightly from above the misshapen nose. Those eyes carried respect and recognition as the Kid's face split with a gap-toothed grin. 'I know you,' he said.

'I don't think so,' Easterly responded in a soft, firm, pleasant tone.

'Why shore,' the giant began. 'I was down to–'

'I've never been there,' the old shootist cut in with a smile that never quite made it to the icy-blue eyes that locked with those of the other man.

Kid Buttercup fell silent as understanding finally registered. 'Yeah,' he said with a shake of the head. 'It weren't you after all – different feller fer sure, amigo. No offence intended, now.'

'None taken,' Easterly replied, and the gratitude in his blue eyes was now obvious to the drifter.

'I'm Kid Buttercup,' the large, buckskin-clad figure announced, stretching out his long arms before resting more easily in the hard wooden chair.

'Joshua Easterly. I own the local hardware store.'

Laughing at his own little sally, the Kid said with a nod in Crenshaw's direction, 'The marshal an' me've already met.' After the three of them fell silent again, Buttercup looked more closely at the badge-toter. 'You lettin' me out at last, marshal?'

'That depends.'

'On what?'

'*Were* you cheatin' at cards?'

'Damn' right, partner.'

'*What?*' Crenshaw gaped in disbelief. 'You *admit* you was cheatin' those men at poker?'

'Damn' straight,' the Kid affirmed. 'It only took me a few hands to see that the tinhorn'd been cheatin' them two cowboys outa their pay. I decided to give him a taste of his own medicine an' then have a real game with them other fellers once I'd run the tinhorn off.' Buttercup rubbed at a sore ear with calloused fingers. 'It jist didn't work out like I planned, is all.'

'*I'll* say it didn't!' The lawman banged the desk with his gnarled fist. 'We got two men laid up at the doc's house an' several more with a variety of injuries.' He held up a hand to silence any protests from the Kid. 'On top of that there's over a hundred dollars' worth of damages at the Silver Slipper got to be paid for, an' you ain't hardly got enough money to get out of town even if I *did* let you go – which I won't.'

'I don't suppose we could jist let bygones be bygones, could we?' the Kid grinned in open good humour. 'No? Ah well, I guess you might as well lock me up again an' bring on lunch, 'cause I'm starved! Now, I don't mean to criticise, Marshal, but that breakfast you served up weren't up to much, an'

I've allus been one to eat a good–'

'We've got an idea,' Easterly cut in, breaking his long silence. The Kid turned his head toward the older man sitting to his left. His brown eyes drifted to the old Colt Navy .36, then back to those icy, sky-blue eyes. Easterly went on, 'We've come up with a way for you to keep out of jail *and* let you work off the money you owe Ned Burdine at the Silver Slipper.'

'Methuselah's ghost!' exclaimed the battered drifter with a chuckle. 'I'm all ears, Josh.'

'You'll work for me,' stated the marshal.

Buttercup's grin began to fade. 'How's that?'

'You'll be a deputy,' clarified Easterly.

'Come again?' The Kid shook his head in confusion as he stuck a dirty finger into his ear as if to clear it of some obstruction.

'I need a temporary deputy,' Crenshaw explained. 'We've had some trouble around here.' In a few brief sentences the lawman told of the crime spree that had swept through the region over the past year and then described the bank robbery that had taken place the previous evening. 'I got to have somebody to help me figure this thing out.' He nodded in the general direction of Easterly. 'Joshua there figures you're the man to give me a hand.'

'You say the bank president was laid out dead in a woman's *dress?*' The grin came back to animate Buttercup's rugged features, but quickly faded once more. 'Sorry, but I ain't interested.'

'We ain't askin'.' Easterly's blue eyes never blinked as the old shootist met the Kid's gaze. 'You do it or you'll stay locked up back there 'till Hell freezes over.'

'Now, hold on there, gents!' Kid Buttercup rose to his feet. He towered over the two older men seated in the small office. 'You can't lock a man up jist fer havin' a little fun!'

Crenshaw met the man's steady stare with a cold gaze of his own and the drifter seemed to lose his sense of humour. 'Watch me.'

'But *I* can't be no deputy!' Buttercup objected, scratching at his stubbly chin. 'Don't you fellers understand? I lie, cheat, steal, drift an' generally get into trouble most every place I go. Now, just how in the name of Methuselah is it gonna look to have a deputy like me? You don't want no cheatin' troublemaker hangin' around town, do you? Iffen I was you, I'd run me outa town fer good!'

'We don't have any choice,' Easterly explained. 'Like it or not, we're gonna have to rely on you to help the marshal out.'

'Ain't nobody can rely on me!' the Kid objected with a hollow, self-conscious laugh. 'Don't you see? I'm a drifter. I play some cards, punch some cattle when I have to, love to fight an' use my .44 an' Bowie when folks get too proddy. I couldn't work fer no lawman! I couldn't *be* no lawman! Hell, my only experience with the law is gettin' locked up fer bein' drunk an' disorderly! Truly,' Buttercup pleaded, 'you fellers jist gotta believe me. I can't be no deputy!'

'It's a deputy or a jail cell,' Crenshaw replied.

'It's a cell,' Easterly added with a grin as he rose to his feet, 'or the badge and–' he began walking for the door '–a drink with me at the Emerald Palace Saloon.'

Kid Buttercup's big-muscled shoulders dropped in resignation. 'Get the badge an' come on,' he said glumly. 'I know when I'm whupped, boys.'

The three men crossed the street to O'Cooners' Emerald Palace. If the giant in buckskins could have known what lay in store for him, then he might well have chosen to remain in jail.

THREE

Easterly, Marshal Crenshaw and Kid Buttercup bellied up to the scarred counter of the Emerald Palace. The hefty form of Gerry O'Cooners held his customary spot behind the bar while scattered patrons occupied a few tables to fill the small tavern with a friendly buzz of conversation. The burly barkeep absently wiped at the battered bartop with a scrap of rag as he listened in on the trio's exchange. The on-going argument had arrived with the three men and the banter brought a broad grin to the Irishman's knocked-around features.

'I *still* say you got the wrong man!' The Kid belted back his second shot of whiskey while Crenshaw and Easterly continued to sip their first. The big man banged his chipped glass down on the counter and added, 'I'll have another!'

'An' I still say ain't none of us got any choice in the matter,' Easterly repeated softly.

'Can't you see I'm a worthless, no-account bum, Marshal?' Buttercup asked, before downing another shot of whiskey in one noisy gulp. 'How can you pin a badge on such a sorry, drunken, brawling, low-life drifter the likes of which stands before you here an' now?' He jerked a thumb at his buckskin-clad chest and pronounced, 'It's disgraceful! That's what it is, boys, jist plumb disgraceful!'

Crenshaw lifted his glass to gently sip the smooth bourbon whiskey. 'It's real simple, Kid, that's what it is. We need help. You might not be much–'

'But you're all we got,' Easterly finished.

O'Cooners filled the Kid's glass with another shot of his worst rotgut whiskey. Without hesitation the giant drained it again before rubbing a calloused palm across his lips. 'I'll have a beer,' he mumbled in disgust.

'Face it,' Crenshaw spoke with the small hint of a grin playing at the corners of his lips. 'You're a deputy. It ain't the end of the world.'

Easterly sipped from his own small glass of bourbon. 'Just do the best you can do and...'

'Crenshaw!' The batwings burst open with a crash as a large figure pushed hurriedly through the scattered sawdust. 'What the hell is goin' on around here, anyway? Is there any semblance of law and order in these parts?'

'Howdy Carl.' The trio turned to face the new arrival. Marshal Crenshaw speaking in level tones. 'What's got you in an uproar this early in the day?'

Carl Winslow crossed the small room in a few long strides to stand before the old star-packer. Winslow stood an even six feet with a solid frame, handsome rugged features, and sandy hair. A colt .45 rode high on his right hip.

'That should be obvious!' Winslow all but

screamed. 'All around us is lawlessness. The bank was robbed last night, and I'm missing cattle from my west range. This whole area is plagued with crime and you want to know what had got me in an uproar!' He punctuated his remarks with an exaggerated sigh of contempt before resuming his tirade. 'Then, instead of finding you on the job, I discover you guzzling booze with trail-trash. *That's* what has me on the boil this morning, Crenshaw!'

Kid Buttercup did not speak, but looked on the confrontation with obvious good humour. Easterly remained silent as well. His attention settled upon the man standing behind and to the left of Carl Winslow. Jay Tippet went everywhere with his boss. Of average size, and nondescript in his cowhand clothing, he seemed no more than a young, dark-haired range-rider. He rarely spoke to anyone except Winslow and most around town regarded him as little more than an extension of his more powerful employer. Joshua Easterly, however, knew better. The two .38 calibre pistols holstered about his hips and the fact that Tippet's hands were never far from their grips, told Easterly everything he needed to know about Winslow's companion. The old shootist knew a killer when he saw one.

'I understand your concern, Carl,' began Crenshaw, 'but–'

'Don't patronise me, Marshal,' Winslow interrupted. 'I want some *results* around here. You've been on the job for almost a year now, and quite frankly I can't see much good in it for Spit Junction. Tell me, Crenshaw, just what do you intend to *do* about all of this?'

'I'm conducting an investigation–'

'With a bottle of whiskey and a couple of drinking buddies?' The belligerent newcomer interrupted the older man once again and Crenshaw heaved an impatient sigh.

'We're lookin' into the bank robbery as best we can.' He took a deliberate sip at the whiskey remaining in his glass. 'As for the cattle, I've told you time and again, I've got nothin' to do with that. I'm town marshal. That means all I can do is notify the county sheriff about the rustling. He'll look into the matter in due time.'

Winslow struggled to bring himself under control. 'I've got a range to manage,' he grated. 'We can't make a profit if the law can't keep rustlers from running off with my cattle. The Box CW is a hard-working outfit, but we've been hit hard by cattle thieves over the past several months, and I've had about all I'm gonna stand of it.'

'I'm sorry, Carl, but that's not in my jurisdiction,' Crenshaw responded with a shake of his head. The old lawman's eyes locked with those of the younger man. 'I'll get a message off to the county sheriff when the stage passes through in a few days. There just ain't nothin' I can do apart from that.' He held his hand to silence the other man's protests. 'Like you say, we got troubles enough right here in town. I've got to get to the bottom of this bank robbery.'

'I can tell you're real busy with that,

Marshal,' the rancher said with heavy sarcasm. Winslow let his gaze travel to the big frame of the reluctant law officer. His eyes came to rest on the grinning, battered features of the man who stood beside the marshal. 'Who's the new deputy?'

'Name's Kid Buttercup.' The giant straightened his large figure to its full height and held out a rough paw in order to shake the other's hand.

Winslow ignored the hand, but met the deputy's eyes with a puzzled look. *'Buttercup?'*

'My favourite flower,' the Kid responded with an ever-widening smile. His hand remained extended and ignored.

The rancher examined the lined face framed within the unruly mass of thick, black hair touched with grey. *'Kid?'* he queried.

'It's an old nickname.' Buttercup laughed out loud, then slapped Winslow on the shoulder with a whack that tumbled him backward a couple of paces. 'Methuselah's ghost! Lighten up, sonny. The day's young and there's still plenty of booze to drink and purty gals to chase! You're too young to be so damn ornery this early in the day, boy!'

Eyes flashing anger, Winslow turned on the marshal once again. 'Was it *your* idea to deputise this big buffoon?'

Easterly spoke now for the first time. 'It was mine.' His icy-blue eyes held the younger man's gaze without blinking, and his tone was soft and gentle in spite of the danger signals in his gaze. 'Can I buy you a drink, Mr Winslow?'

'No.' The rancher's mouth went dry, so that the word was raspy. Though he hated to confess it, even to himself, those cold eyes stirred fear deep in his belly. Involuntarily he took another step back toward the door. Jay Tippet held his ground, standing relaxed and unmoving. 'Some other time, maybe. I've got to be headin' on back out to the Box CW...' He turned quickly and strode from the room. Tippet let a bitter smile animate his features for a brief moment, then followed in his employer's wake.

'Friendly feller.' Kid Buttercup turned back to the counter to drain the beer mug before him. 'How 'bout another of them cool, sudsy beers, pardner?' O'Cooners filled the tall mug and the Kid emptied the brew in three long gulps, then followed the act with the request to, 'keep 'em comin', old hoss.'

'Never did care for Carl Winslow,' Easterly observed quietly as he turned back to the counter. 'He's a pushy young pup.'

'Sure now, that one's been on a high horse ever since he turned up here a couple of years back,' O'Cooners observed. 'He bought up quite a few of the locals to put together that Box CW spread and he's lorded it over his neighbours ever since.'

'Always have had trouble with that hardcase crew of his,' Crenshaw muttered, finishing off the shot of bourbon in his glass and refusing a second from the bottle proffered by the Irishman. He's got more'n a dozen of the roughest cowhands I've run across in a good long while.'

'They're a rowdy bunch, that's a fact,' Easterly nodded, draining his glass. 'That Tippet bears some watching as well.' He locked eyes with Kid Buttercup. For a brief, serious moment the giant gave a slight dip of his chin to indicate his understanding before letting go with a loud, boisterous laugh. The deputy held out his empty mug to O'Cooners.

'Great galloping Methuselah's ghost!' the Kid bellowed with an infectious grin. 'Don't let that sour-tempered jasper spoil all the fun. Drink up!' He raised yet another mug of beer to his lips with delight.

While Buttercup's Adam's apple bobbed in a frenzy, O'Cooners expressed growing concern over his fiancée's safety. 'You'll be after understanding me worries about the well-being of that lovely, gentle little lady who'll be me bride in a few more days,' he said, looking from Easterly to Crenshaw. 'There's been much skulduggery about these parts the past year or more and it's getting too close to home, me lads; *much* too close to home.'

'She'll be OK,' the old shootist reassured his friend. 'They hit the stage recently, so they'll leave it be for a while anyway. Don't fret, Gerry. She's made it all the way from Ireland. She can make it to Spit Junction by stage, and that's for certain.'

'You say this little girl is comin' all the way from Ireland to marry you, O'Cooners?' Crenshaw asked with a grin. 'That's hard for me to believe.'

'She's a beauty,' the big bartender said, adding with a wink at his companions, 'and a saint of a lady who knows how to be a divil of a woman.'

Kid Buttercup's eyes took on the twinkle of the contrary prankster as he slammed the empty mug back to the counter for another refill. 'How long since you seen this gal, hoss?'

'I've not seen me intended for six years now, bucko,' the Irishman answered with the light of love in his eyes. 'But I know she's as beautiful today as the day I left her on the soil of Ireland.'

'Hell, Irish,' the Kid slapped the counter top with a big, open palm. 'That woman's done got fat, sassy, grey and frazzled. She waited on you so long that the uglies had plumb set in on her, *that's* why she crossed the ocean – to find the only man that'll have her.'

'That's not funny, you dim-witted son of a jackass!' O'Cooners roared his disapproval, so that everyone in the tavern took notice, 'She's a fine filly from the auld country and I'll have you show some respect or I'll…'

'Sure, old hoss, sure.' Buttercup burped loudly. 'Why she's a purty as me, I bet. No doubt about it.'

'Why, you–' The Irishman began to come around the bar with knotted fists clenched. A fighter he had been and there was no fear in the red-headed barkeep.

Crenshaw blocked the man's path with his own body. 'Settle down, Gerry. The Kid's only funnin' with you.'

'Come on.' Easterly grabbed Buttercup by

the arm. 'It's time for us to go.'

'I'll break the man in pieces with me bare hands!' O'Cooners raved as the lawman held him back. 'Slander me beloved, will he? Why I've a mind to...'

'He was only kiddin',' the marshal said, gripping the bartender with strong hands. 'Take it easy, Gerry.'

'Just a joke, pardner.' The Kid waved a big hand and grinned as Easterly hustled him out through the batwings. 'Ain't you got no sense of humour?' The giant laughed as he and the old gunfighter waited in front of the small saloon for Crenshaw. 'Crazy Irishman,' he mumbled as his laughter rumbled to a halt.

'That man came close to being the boxing champion of the world,' Easterly pointed out. 'I'd go easy on him if I were you, Kid. You might bite off a bit more'n you could chew.'

'It *could* happen, old pard, but then again, I'm a mighty big chewer. You know, I was once–' Kid Buttercup stopped in mid-sentence with his jaw hanging slack. The starpacker had joined them at last, so that he and Easterly followed the big hulk's stupefied gaze with interest of their own. 'Ain't that the most beautifullest woman you ever laid eyes on, fellers? Why, she's purtier than a yucca flower in full bloom!'

'That's the new schoolmarm,' Crenshaw grinned in appreciation. 'She's a sight, and that's a fact.' He paused a minute, then added, 'Joshua here married the school-teacher afore this one. She's a right purty gal herself.'

'Well, iffen she's any finer than this here darlin' lady, then that old man better lock her up to keep her safe, 'cause ol' Kid Buttercup is on the prowl!' The Kid almost drooled, but his tongue swiped across his lips instead.

'Close your mouth and mind your manners,' Easterly cautioned, elbowing the big man sharply. 'She's lookin' this way, you big, ugly oaf.'

The lady in question stood barely five feet

tall and weighed no more than a hundred pounds. Bright red hair set off a pale, lightly freckled complexion. She had a fresh, scrubbed appearance of healthy, natural beauty complimented by a shapely figure that included pronounced curves in all the proper places. Even at a distance, she was an impressive young woman.

'Have mercy, Marshal!' Buttercup exploded. 'You could lock me up jist fer what I'm thinkin'!'

Another elbow to the Kid's ribs silenced the big man, while Easterly shifted the topic of conversation to the lady's companion. 'What you reckon she's talking to him for, Jack? That's an unlikely pair if ever I saw one.'

The attractive schoolmarm stood on the boardwalk in front of the general store, talking with Carl Winslow while Jay Tippet loafed in deceptive idleness off to the side. Quickly, the rancher tipped his hat to the lady before hurrying off down the street while the young lady made her way toward the trio assembled before the Emerald Palace. Her steps seemed firm and determined.

'Ain't no doubt in my rusty old brain what Winslow's got on his mind, boys,' the Kid spoke up. 'He ain't no different from me nor any other man when it comes to a beautiful woman. Hell's bells on a ring-tailed bobcat, any feller in his right mind would stop to talk to that gal if he met her on the street!'

Easterly's elbow once again punched sharply at the big man, bringing a grunt of pain. 'Shut up and behave yourself, Kid!'

As the school teacher approached, the trio could see a look of disapproval set upon her lovely features.

'Marshal,' she said in soft, cultured tones, 'I'd appreciate a moment of your time, please.'

'Certainly, Miss Martha,' Crenshaw replied, tipping his stetson to the lady. 'You know Easterly.' She nodded slightly in the direction of the silver-haired hardware store owner. 'Let me introduce my temporary deputy, Kid Buttercup.'

'Pleased to make your acquaintance, Mr–'

'Just call me, Kid,' the Kid smiled broadly as he swept his own hat from the top of his head. 'I'm honoured to meet you, Miss Martha.'

'Martha Dorsett,' the young lady added. Her eyes locked with those of Kid Buttercup and he read welcome signs that the others did not see. The woman shifted her attention back to the lawman. 'Now, Marshal Crenshaw…'

'Yes, Miss Martha? What can I do for you?'

'There's simply far too much criminal activity in our community.' The little lady spoke in firm, soft tones that carried the conviction of youth. 'Why we had that dreadful bank robbery last evening and now Mr Winslow informs me that cattle are being taken from his range. We really must have protection from the lawless element.'

'We're workin' on it, Miss Martha,' the marshal replied as he fidgeted with a loose button on his shirt. 'We'll get to the bottom of these problems, ma'am, I promise you.'

'When I agreed to come to your community, I was assured that this was a law-abiding, God-fearing town of solid citizens. You advertised for a proper lady school-teacher and I responded to that request in good faith. I came here expecting to live at peace with my neighbours and to be safe from sordid ruffians. If this type of thing continues...'

'Miss Martha,' Kid Buttercup interrupted, 'you have my personal promise that law an' order will once again reign supreme in this fair city. Why, just this very mornin' I done volunteered my services as a special deputy whose sworn duty is to restore peace an' tranquillity to this lovely community. Fair maiden, take heart an' be of good cheer, for I–'

'Oh shuddap!' Easterly's elbow connected with the giant's ribs with a resounding thud, but Miss Martha seemed impressed by the Kid's reassuring words.

'I thank you, Mr Kid,' she said, once again meeting the big man's stare, and causing icy water to slip down the drifter's lengthy spine so that he had to stifled a sudden shiver of anticipation.

'I'll be lookin' after your safety an' happiness, Miss Martha,' the Kid said, bowing slightly from the waist. 'You can count on me for your every need.'

'Good day, Marshal,' the schoolteacher turned to leave. 'Mr Easterly.' She nodded at the silver-haired man. 'I feel better already, just knowing that Mr Kid Buttercup is on the job.'

'I've done died an' gone to Heaven,' Buttercup whispered as he walked away. He scratched one armpit and belched with obvious satisfaction. 'I'm in love.'

'You're disgustin'.' Easterly growled as he stalked off in the direction of his hardware store, his bootheels stirring dust along the hard-packed earth that fronted the stores and businesses. The marshal and his new deputy remained behind.

'Come on,' Crenshaw grinned. 'We got work to do, "Mr Kid Buttercup".' The lawman paused briefly. 'What is your name, anyway? This Kid Buttercup stuff gets pretty old.'

Buttercup suddenly stared down at the toes of his scuffed boots. He kicked at a dirt clod that crumbled upon impact. 'I ain't tellin'. It ain't important…'

'I bet Joshua and O'Cooners know,' Crenshaw observed. 'They know just about everybody and everything around these parts.'

'Aw hell,' the Kid complained, still shuffling about. 'My mama called me Elwood W. Kirklymoore. The "W" ain't nothin' but a letter, there's no middle name. You happy now?'

Crenshaw's laugh brought a pink glow to the Kid's weathered features. 'Jeez, what a moniker!' The lawman began steps towards his office. 'On second thoughts, I do believe we'll stick with Kid Buttercup.'

'Suits me,' came the reply from the big man following close behind. 'Don't know 'bout you, Marshal, but me, I'm ready for some lunch.' He burped loudly, then wiped a hand across his mouth. 'All that beer done give me a case of gas.'

'Work first,' the marshal said as the Kid trailed along with a heavy, shambling gait. 'Lunch later.'

'Suit yourself,' the giant replied, scratching the bristles on his chin. 'I've been hungry before.'

Marshal and deputy progressed on to the law office, then disappeared through the open doorway. From the shadows across the street, Ned Burdine watched with unconcealed animosity.

FOUR

Easterly sat at the kitchen table, enjoying a final cup of hot black coffee before leaving for church with his wife and son. Betty was off in the back bedroom, completing her own preparations and dressing the baby for Sunday service. Sipping at the thick, bitter brew, the old gunman heard an insistent pounding at the kitchen door. He pulled at the starched white collar fitting snug about his neck, then quickly sprang to his feet to step off the space that separated him from the door. The thunderous banging came again, but this time it was accompanied by an equally thunderous voice.

'You gonna open up this door, or let a poor man stand out to catch his chill in the mornin' air?'

The query, roared out in all-too-recognisable tones, brought a good-natured groan from Joshua. It seemed that Kid Buttercup had that effect on folks.

Easterly opened the door with a faint grin animating his features. 'You plan on comin' to Sunday service with us?' he enquired. 'Or are you just knockin' my door down for the exercise?'

He stepped aside to let the big man stomp into the small warm kitchen. The newly-appointed deputy quickly settled his large frame into one of the empty chairs at the oak table. 'Thought you might be sociable an' ask a poor stranger to breakfast,' the Kid responded bluntly. 'I figgered, what with you havin' a purty woman an' all, you might jist see your way clear to–'

'We ate more'n an hour ago, Kid,' Easterly informed his uninvited guest. 'Howsomever, there's a few biscuits left over, an' plenty of coffee.'

'Bring it on, old hoss!' Kid Buttercup snatched a fluffy biscuit from the platter before his host could even place it on the table in front of him. As the drifter packed away the leftover biscuits, Easterly poured him a big mug of hot coffee, then resumed his seat across the table. He watched the big man eat a half-dozen biscuits smeared with butter and heaped high with fruit preserves before attempting to engage the deputy in further conversation.

'Now,' Easterly began. 'Were you plannin' on goin' to service with Betty, Wheeler an' me?'

'What kinda service be that?' Buttercup asked with a raised eyebrow and an absent-minded scratch at one armpit.

'We got Sunday service down at the school-house with the local Methodist congregation,' Easterly explained patiently. 'There's a preacher that comes through here about once every–'

'Naw!' The Kid shook his head, then gulped down a mouthful of hot, black brew. 'I'm a born-again-dunk-'em-deep Baptist. I don't hold with no sprinklin' babies an' sich as that there.'

'So,' the older man said, changing the subject to hide his amusement over the notion of the big range-rider being any particular brand of churchgoer, 'what brings you by here this early in the mornin', Kid?'

'Jus' thought I'd ask you a few questions, Joshua,' Kid Buttercup replied between large swallows of coffee. 'For example, I'm curious about this here Burdine feller. What can you tell me about his doin's in these parts?'

'What's there to tell?' answered Easterly, sipping his own coffee quietly. 'He come to town a couple of years back an' opened up the Silver Slipper. It's the fanciest, most high-falutin' waterin'-hole in the whole area. He's a cantankerous cuss, but–'

'But nothin'!' interrupted Buttercup. 'I never did trust no saloon-owner an' gamblin' man. He's been after my hide over that little ruckus I had over to his place, an' I think he jist might be the snake we're lookin' fer in all this foolishness hereabouts.'

Easterly continued to sip quietly at his

coffee before observing in soft, measured tones, 'You can think anythin' you like.' He followed that with a pause, designed to add emphasis to his next words. 'But you got to have some proof before you do anythin' about it, Kid.'

'That's jist exactly what I aim to find!' The big man in the fringed buckskins pushed himself erect from the chair. 'I think I'll mosey over to that Silver Slipper Saloon an' see if I can scare up another cup o' coffee on this bright mornin'.'

'Stay out of trouble, Deputy,' Easterly advised as his new companion opened the kitchen door. 'Burdine ain't exactly partial to your company.'

'Trouble?' Kid Buttercup stared innocently into the sky-blue eyes of the older man. 'I can't imagine what you is talkin' about, old pard.'

Before any further words could be exchanged, the reluctant lawman was through the doorway and closing the portal behind him with a house-shaking bang. Betty

Easterly shouted some exclamation from the bedroom which caused the gunman to grin and be thankful that the circuit-riding Methodist preacher had not stopped by for breakfast as he sometimes did on Sunday mornings. He wondered just how long it would take for the explosion to ignite at the Silver Slipper.

Ned Burdine sat moodily in the most distant corner of his elaborate saloon. An old man shuffled about the sawdust-covered floor, cleaning tables and emptying brass spittoons, while a lone bartender polished glasses behind the ornate counter. The big bouncer, Otto Wendt, was slumped in a corner across the room from his employer, catching a mid-morning nap in the warm sunshine streaming through a spotless front window.

Burdine's fancy saloon had never quite been the draw he had hoped for, but neither could he exactly call the place a failure. Certainly the gambler and saloon-owner made money. But for some reason he had yet to lure away the established clientele of the faded Emerald Palace. He wondered just what appeal Gerry O'Cooners' place held for the drinking men of this little town. No, in addition to his less-than-spectacular business profits, he was making a loss due to the damage from that brawl two nights previously. Times were not shining for Ned Burdine. Sometimes he wondered why he had ever left New Orleans. He sipped absently at a cup of hot tea while he contemplated his lack of good fortune.

The doors that fronted Main Street opened with a bang. Burdine shifted his eyes to the big man who pushed through the doorway with the chill fall breeze following him in off the wide, dusty street. A scowl turned the gambler's handsome face hard as he pushed back his chair and rose quickly to his feet.

'We're not open yet,' he growled to the newcomer.

'Sure you're open,' Kid Buttercup boomed

with his best grin in place. 'Your door's unlocked, ain't it? 'Sides, all I'm lookin' fer is a cup o' hot coffee.'

'This isn't a café, Deputy,' Burdine replied with an edge to his voice. 'Come back later, when we're open for business. Or better still, don't come back at *all*.'

'I think you're open *now*, Burdine.' The bartender put a mug of coffee into the big man's hand: he wanted no trouble from the stranger who'd smashed up the saloon and a small army of local cowboys. 'I have some business with you, whether you like it or not,' the Kid continued. The grin remained in place, but did not travel as far as his eyes. He tapped a blunt, dirty finger at the tarnished star pinned to his greasy buckskin shirt.

'Yeah, yeah,' the saloon-owner snarled in disgust. 'I heard all about that lazy old lawman appointing you as his deputy. I'd say you two make a good pair.' He shook his head in exaggerated amusement. 'There's certainly no one with less intelligence in the whole damn county than our local law-enforcement team, and that's a fact!'

Buttercup gulped the steaming brew with a loud slurp before he winked an eye at Burdine, then asked a question. 'Jist where was you this past Friday night, Mr Burdine? I mean o' course, when that bank was bein' robbed?'

'Any idiot – and that does include you – would know where I am on *any* night of the week; right here at the Silver Slipper. Just what do you think you're doing, anyway? You can't just come into my place of business and–'

'I suppose you can prove your story?' the Kid queried between slurps.

'I don't have to prove *anything* to you or that bumbling fool of a marshal.' Burdine's voice rose from a growl to a shout. 'Now get out of my saloon before I have you thrown out by the seat of your pants.'

'You feel up to that this early in the mornin', Mr Burdine?' If anything, Buttercup's smile showed even wider than before.

'You ready for a little Sunday mornin' recreation?'

'I don't *have* to be,' Burdine replied with a sly grin replacing the angry scowl that corrugated his handsome face. 'I simply stand aside and enjoy the festivities.'

'I'll say it straight, Burdine,' the bigger man remarked, draining his coffee mug in a final swallow before banging it down on the bar. 'You turn up here an' suddenly there's murder an' robbery all over the Panhandle.' Buttercup roared now as he leant forward and grabbed a handful of the smaller man's starched shirtfront, 'I think there's somethin' shady about you, an' I'm gonna keep an eye on things hereabouts.'

'You'll regret this, trail-scum,' Burdine snarled.

'I don't think you're man enough to *make* me.' The deputy released his captive with a small shove. 'Come ahead if you like.'

A new voice entered into the heated exchange. This one was calm, flat and devoid of emotion. It said, 'That's *my* job.'

'I was afraid of that,' observed Kid Buttercup as he shifted his gaze to find Otto Wendt standing ten feet away. 'You wouldn't want to jist let this pass, would you, old hoss? I mean now, you an' me got nothin' to be fightin' about, Otto ol' pard.'

The bouncer moved to close the gap that separated him from his adversary. 'Put 'em up,' he growled.

'I kinda thought you'd say that,' muttered the Kid as he stepped forward to land a big punch smack on Otto's granite jaw.

Later – much, much later – Kid Buttercup would remember that the punch had landed solid on the giant's chin. He felt that blow clear down to the tips of his boots and his hand ached for hours afterward. He knew the punch had landed clean and hard. He just did not understand why Otto never seemed to feel the damned thing. Otto Wendt never blinked an eye.

Kid Buttercup had the peculiar sensation of flying. This was not unusual, since the bouncer had easily lifted and then tossed the deputy across the room. The flight was brief, however, and ended with a bone-jarring bounce from a nearby wall. The Kid remembered wondering briefly if this was the origin of the term 'bouncer' then quickly shook the thought from his ringing head.

Scrambling to his feet, Buttercup met the German's ponderous advance with a savage jab followed by a powerful right hook that glanced off the hard, shaved skull of the behemoth before him. A straight right from the bouncer seemed to further confuse the deputy's already twisted nose, while a left hook exploded in his ear with a force that brought the sound of multiple bells echoing in his skull.

Kid Buttercup forced a grin as he held his hands before him in a gesture designed to halt the attack. 'Otto, old hoss,' he panted. 'I think you got me, pard. I'll slip out quietly an' there'll be no hard feelin's.'

Wendt slowly took a step back, grinning in victory. The Kid used the opportunity to unleash a kick to the tender area between the giant's legs while grasping a chair that he splintered over the German's head and shoulders. His face broke into a wide smile as he stepped back to watch the big bouncer fall to the floor.

'*Timber!*' Buttercup shouted.

'Not fair,' is all Otto said in reply.

His big looping right hand came from somewhere near the floor. Kid Buttercup never saw it coming, but it wouldn't have mattered even if he had. After the punch landed, Otto simply tossed the rumpled deputy out the front door. Marshal Crenshaw found the battered figure in the windswept street five minutes later. The Kid's nose was leaking crimson. The Kid himself was sitting in a daze, still wondering how it could be that one man could pack so much power into a single punch.

'Methuselah's ghost!' the Kid exclaimed after downing his fifth beer of the evening. 'That man can *hit!*'

He had slept most of the afternoon before

joining Marshal Crenshaw, Joshua Easterly and Gerry O'Cooners at the Emerald Palace. Four shots of whiskey and five beers later, the deputy was beginning to feel something like his old self again.

'I told you to stay out of trouble,' Easterly reminded him. 'Burdine ain't nobody to mess with, an' for sure Otto Wendt ain't the kinda man *I'd* hunt up for a playmate.'

'That's a fact,' Crenshaw agreed, eyeing the blue and purple colouration marking his deputy's features. 'You might consider steerin' clear of that German bouncer if you value your good health.'

Buttercup gently touched his nose, then rubbed at his tender jaw. 'You won't have to tell me twice,' he promised. 'But I still say that Burdine is up to somethin'.'

Crenshaw began to protest. 'Just 'cause he's an ornery cuss don't necessarily mean that—'

'Well, tell me *this,* then,' interrupted the deputy. 'Jist where *was* Burdine and his pet gorilly on Friday night, when that bank was bein' robbed?'

'They was at the Silver Slipper, Kid,' Crenshaw answered with a small shake of the head. 'Burdine told me you asked him that this mornin'.'

'A-ha!' Buttercup lifted a soiled finger to the ceiling. 'That proves the man's a liar fer damn' sure. We had that little ruckus down to his saloon that Friday, but Burdine an' Otto weren't nowheres to be found. Now, what do you think o' *that,* lawdog?'

'I think you're jumpin' to conclusions, Kid,' the old starpacker announced with a grin. 'When that brawl of yours took place late Friday afternoon, Burdine and Wendt were over to the café, eatin' supper just like they always do before business picks up in the evenin'. They were back at the Silver Slipper before the bank closed for the night.'

Kid Buttercup's face turned a gentle shade of crimson and he floundered for a moment, then broke out in a loud bluster, 'Well, I *still* say he's got somethin' to hide, or my name ain't–'

'Elwood W Kirklymoore,' O'Cooners finished, joining in the round of laughter that suddenly surrounded the deputy.

'Where'd you hear that?' Buttercup sputtered in bug-eyed surprise. 'Who told you that?'

'Word gets around,' the barkeep remarked with a wink at Easterly and Crenshaw. 'It *is* your name, after all, Mr Kirklymoore.'

'I goes by Kid Buttercup an' you knows it!' exploded the drifter. Then a shifty look came to the big man's eyes and he man-ouevred to change the topic of conversation. 'You'd best have your fun while you can, you big Irish 'tater.'

The grin quickly faded from the bar-tender's face. 'What you gettin' at, Kid?'

'Soon as that three hunnerd pound hell-cat gets here from old Ireland, you'll be losin' that sense o' humour fer good,' Buttercup predicted with a grin of his own. He watched the colour rise to the Irishman's face, then added, 'I jist hope her moustache don't tickle too much when you two kiss.'

'I'll take him apart with me bare hands!' O'Cooners roared as Easterly and Crenshaw leapt to restrain him. The big barkeep was coming over the counter at the Kid, but the lawman and the hardware owner somehow managed to keep him firmly in their grasp.

'Get outa here, will you, Kid?' growled the marshal. 'We got enough trouble as it is, without you stirrin' up O'Cooners here with your foolishness.'

Buttercup drained his sixth beer before heading for the door. 'I'm jist tryin' to forewarn the poor feller is all. Couple days from now, when that stagecoach pulls in from St Louis, he'll be sorry. Hell, he'll likely be on the next stage *outa* here once he gets a look at the beast from old Ireland.'

The bartender's obscenities filled the air of the small drinking establishment, matched only by the loud, roaring laughter of Kid Buttercup as he exited the Emerald Palace to turn toward the marshal's office where he intended to bed down for the night on the sagging old couch. A half-dozen purposeful strides in that direction were stopped short by the sound of lead smacking into the wall near his head, followed closely by the sharp report of a rifle.

Buttercup quickly made a head-first leap to land behind the shelter of a nearby water barrel. His eyes began searching for the source of the shot. He was not disappointed as the rifle sound twice more and two lead slugs slapped the wooden slats of the barrel behind which he had taken shelter.

The muzzle flashes gave the deputy a target. He squeezed the trigger on the big Remington .44, but the sound of running feet was the only response. Quickly Kid Buttercup became the pursuer as he leapt to his feet and gave chase.

Someone shouted a question from the doorway of the Emerald Palace. 'What's going on?'

'*Come on!*' replied the big drifter as he pounded after the retreating rifleman. 'He's gettin' away from us!'

As Buttercup entered the dark, narrow space that separated the two buildings, he had to pause for a moment to listen for the would-be killer's footsteps. He heard them off to his left, then took off once again in pursuit. Rounding the corner into the back alley, he saw a shadowy figure with a rifle stumble over a pile of discarded rubbish. The resulting racket would have awakened the dead and the Kid added to the noise by firing a shot that smacked into a large metal can near the floundering form that sprawled among the scattered trash.

'Hold it right there, you bustard!' Deputy Buttercup boomed. 'Next one'll put an extry hole through your head!'

The figure dropped the rifle while scrambling upright, then shoved hands above his head in a gesture of surrender. Kid Buttercup heard the sound of running feet approaching from the rear. He suspected that Easterly and Crenshaw would join him in moments.

Just then, a door opened along the back alley. Light streamed into the rubbish-lined pathway. Two figures with guns in hand stepped from the brightly lit doorway to stand between the Kid and his quarry. Both had guns trained in the direction of the big lawman.

'Get outa the way, damn you!' Buttercup yelled.

'Drop that gun!' came the response.

Buttercup realised with some surprise that it was Ned Burdine levelling a pistol at him. Before he could do or say anything, the saloon-owner demanded, 'What are you doing out here, anyway?'

Otto Wendt had a double-barrelled scatter-gun pointed at the lawman, while Burdine's revolver remained fixed upon his chest. They were powerful reasons to answer the saloon-owner's question calmly and reasonably. But Kid Buttercup wasn't always long on calmness *or* reason.

'You damn idjit!' he roared. 'I said get outa the way!'

Seeing the man he had cornered quickly and quietly slipping away between buildings just before the marshal and the old shootist turned the corner to approach the trio engaged in a back-alley Mexican stand-off the Kid shouted in frustration, 'He's gettin' *away*, dagblastit!'

'What is this buffoon talking about, Marshal?' Burdine asked as he tucked the small revolver into the holster beneath his shoulder. Otto lowered the shotgun as the elder lawman and his companion arrived on the scene. 'We saw no one but this fool out here in a dark alley shooting off his weapon and making a racket.'

'I was chasin' a man what shot at me from ambush, you dim-witted son of an armadillo!' Buttercup cried, trembling in fury. 'I had him covered when you and Attila the Hun come out your back door and let him git away!' The deputy shoved his .44 into the worn holster on his left hip. 'Had it all planned out, didn't you, Burdine? Hire a feller to git rid of me, then, when your plan fails, you helps him make good his getaway!'

'I don't have to stand here and take that kind of accusation!' Burdine protested indignantly, only to be interrupted by a new-comer who stood in the lighted doorway.

'Mr Burdine has been with me most of the evening, Marshal.'

Carl Winslow's form was framed by the yellow light from the back door of the Silver Slipper Saloon. Jay Tippet stood beside and slightly behind his employer. 'We heard the racket, so Ned and Otto came out to investi-gate. That's all there is to it.'

'You ain't gonna believe that story are you, Jack?' Buttercup waved his arms about as he screamed into the dark. 'This tinhorn is up to no good!'

'You'll not insult me, you saddle-trash. Why, I...'

'That's enough from both of you!' Crenshaw snapped sharply. 'I don't want to hear it!'

'But, Jack, I tell you...' spluttered the Kid.

'Oh, shut up!' Crenshaw turned on his

heel, then flung back over his shoulder, 'Tell me about it over breakfast in the morning – and not before!'

With a shrug, Easterly followed his friend back toward the Emerald Palace. Burdine and the others quickly disappeared back through the door of Burdine's saloon.

'Well, I'll be sheep-dipped!' exclaimed Kid Buttercup. He rubbed at his aching jaw, then stalked off in an angry mood toward a night's rest at the jailhouse.

FIVE

'I still say that slick polecat from the Silver Slipper's mixed up in all these shenanigans around here!'

Kid Buttercup somehow managed to squeeze his words out around a mouthful of sausage. He washed the food down with a swallow of scalding black coffee that he then placed back on the table beside his piled breakfast plate. 'I had that bushwhacker nailed dead to rights las' night – before that Burdine *hombre* let him git away from me. You can't tell me that was no accident!'

'And you can't prove a thing,' Marshal Crenshaw reminded him with as much patience as he could muster. 'Until you've got something you can prove, you ain't got nothin' you can arrest him for, so you might as well keep all your dagblasted suspicions to your ownself. We been listening to your tales all mornin', Kid, but they ain't movin' us one step closer to solvin' any of the things we're up against.'

Buttercup, Crenshaw and Joshua Easterly were engaged in an early breakfast on a bright, clear Monday morning at the small Good Food Café off a short side street in the centre of town. The tiny eaterie held only half a dozen tables along with five seats lining a small counter, but the food was good and the coffee hot. The marshal and his headstrong deputy had been over the events of the previous evening more times than any of them could recall. Throughout these recitations of the ambush and chase, the trio seemed to be making little progress beyond the Kid's stubborn insistence that Burdine and Wendt were somehow involved in the attack upon him.

'But I tell you, that no-good Burdine was–' the big man began again as he stuffed a fluffy biscuit into his open mouth. He chewed the words along with his food so that it all came out a garbled mess of biscuit and verbiage.

'Let's move on to somethin' else,' Easterly suggested with an easy tone. 'Whatever happened last night is one small piece in a much bigger puzzle. What began as scattered robberies is rapidly growin' into a nasty pattern that's hit Spit Junction hard. I can only guess that them shots fired at you yest'day evening was tied in with your efforts at investigatin' the bank robbery. That is, if we can find the scalawag at the bottom of all these hold-ups, then I'm bettin' we'll find the feller that's responsible for firin' them shots last night.'

Buttercup chewed mightily while nodding his head in agreement. Crenshaw sipped thoughtfully at his coffee cup. The silver-haired shootist continued with his observations after pouring himself another cup of coffee from the pot resting in the centre of the small table.

'Now, we know there's been a whole string of stick-ups an' such all over the area these past two years or so,' Easterly recalled for the little assemblage. 'Our most immediate trouble is the bank robbery here in town, but I have an idea all this is tied up together. Furthermore, I don't think it's any coincidence that Spit Junction's been quiet up until now. I think the outlaw band that's responsible holes up near here, and that's why they've laid off Spit Junction over the past several months an' probably figgered nobody around here would be sharp enough to pick on 'em.' He paused for a moment, took a drink from his coffee cup and then continued, 'What we got to think over is just who might be involved; 'who's moved into the area in the past couple of years?'

'There's Burdine!' blurted Buttercup, undeterred by a mouth stuffed full of scrambled eggs. 'He an' that Otto Wendt fit the bill jus' fine!'

'Give it up,' groaned Crenshaw.

'OK, there's Burdine,' agreed the old gunman with a grin. 'But there's also Carl Winslow. He's been a pretty hard-nosed character with a tough crew out on that big

Box CW spread of his. I ain't real certain just why he always seems to have so many hardcase cowboys on his payroll with so few head of cattle to account for on all that range of his. An' let's not forget Jay Tippet, either. If you ask me, Winslow and that crowd are worth lookin' at for sure. There's things that just don't add up there.'

'Yeah,' Buttercup agreed. 'And he was with Burdine last night. I bet they's both in cahoots on the whole deal.'

Easterly ignored the deputy who returned to shovelling food into his perpetually chewing mouth. 'Was there any CW hands in town the night of the bank robbery, Jack? Did anybody see anything of Winslow or his crew Friday evening?'

'Hell,' Crenshaw growled, 'there's almost always a few of them Box CW boys in town on just about any night of the week. Yeah, there was some of Winslow's crew hanging around the Silver Slipper that night. 'Fact, when I questioned O'Cooners after the robbery, he said he saw a couple of the boys stumbling down the street with a gal from Burdine's place when he was lockin' up a little after midnight. They was kinda laughin' real quiet-like and passin' a bottle back and forth between them. You know how them cowboys are when they get a little liquor and a gal to go along with 'em. They were just havin' some fun.' Crenshaw winked at his companions. 'I suppose the last thing them boys had on their minds was robbin' a bank.'

Buttercup slurped hot coffee and chuckled at the same time – the two activities taken together produced a loud gurgling noise that seemed to amuse the big man all the more. He too imagined the cowhands in question were not thinking about bank robbery as they ambled down the darkened street with a bottle of whiskey and a girl between them.

'Then there's this business of Orson T Philbertt found dead, dressed like a woman an' locked in his own bank vault with the keys in his pocket and everything locked up tight as a drum from the outside.' Easterly shook his head in confusion then sipped idly at his coffee. 'This one'd worry the horns off a billy goat.'

'Old Orson was never quite the same after his wife passed on here a year or so back,' Crenshaw observed. 'He fired the servants and lived there all alone in that big house just a couple of blocks down from the bank. Why in heaven's name he was dressed up in them women's clothes is a question I sure want answered while we're doin' all this here detective work. It just ain't proper for a man to go out that way.'

'That's a fact,' Deputy Buttercup agreed solemnly.

'You'll get no argument from me on that point,' Easterly added. 'But what does all this add up to? There's got to be some way these pieces start fitting together. Any ideas?' He held up his hands to halt a rush of words from the Kid. 'Anything, that is, other than your thoughts on Ned Burdine.'

'Well…' The deputy struggled for something fresh to say. 'Is there anybody else new around town?'

'There's that pretty little schoolmarm,' Crenshaw suggested, laughing at his own joke. 'But this ain't exactly a boom town. We're smack in the middle of the Texas Panhandle with nothin' but miles of cattle and grassland around us. Other than driftin' cow hands, there just ain't that many folks movin' in and out of here. I think we've about covered 'em.'

'I think I'll ride on out to the Box CW to ask a few questions later this mornin',' Kid Buttercup announced after draining his coffee cup. 'Sweet Petunia needs to get out fer to stretch her legs a bit anyhow, so's I might as well jist poke around out there to see what Carl Winslow has got to say fer hisself.'

'I'll tell you again,' Easterly interjected. 'Stay out of trouble, Kid.'

'Me?' Buttercup's exaggerated innocence amused neither the marshal nor the hardware store owner. 'Why I ain't got no hankerin' fer no trouble whatsoever. That sort of thing is the furtherest from my mind, boys.'

The Kid pushed to his feet, said his good-byes and made for the door while the two older men remained seated at the table, enjoying their final cup of coffee. As Buttercup stepped outside, closing the door behind him, he spotted Martha Dorsett walking briskly along the other side of the wide main street.

'Miss Dorsett!' The big deputy boomed in his thunderous voice. 'Mornin' to you ma'am!' He set out to cross the road while waving and grinning at the young woman who stood quietly examining the buckskin-clad figure stomping towards her with all the grace of a bull ox.

'Good morning to you, Mr Kid Buttercup, sir.' Martha Dorsett's warm smile and exaggerated greeting gave a boost to the drifter's morale as he approached the schoolteacher and swiped a sleeve across his mouth to remove the remainder of his breakfast. 'I can't tell you how good it is to see you alert and on patrol. A young lady feels safer just knowing that you are keeping your eye on things here in our town.'

'Well now, darlin', you can shore 'nuff count on old Kid Buttercup.' Without Easterly there to make him mind his manners, the deputy decided to turn up the charm just to see how far it would take him. 'Why now, you're about as purty a young thang as I've seen in quite some time, honey. I don't suppose a gal like you would let a feller sich as me go walkin' with you nor nothin' like that now, would you, sweet thang?'

'Of course not, Mr Kid Buttercup.' Martha Dorsett watched the battered features of the big man seemingly melt from ear to ear grin to hang-dog frown. 'However,' she added, lowering her voice to conspiratorial tones and meeting his gaze with a searching look of her own, 'If you would be so kind as to stop by my home tomorrow evening, then I could offer you a home-cooked meal.' She paused briefly, while a small, pink tongue moistened her full lips. 'I can only assume that a gentleman such as yourself can keep his romantic encounters strictly confidential? After all, this is a small town and people could, ah, *talk*.'

The Kid swallowed hard as he nodded in vigorous response to her query. He read an open invitation in the schoolteacher's beautiful eyes. 'Yes ma'am,' he croaked.

'Well then – handsome,' the young woman said with a smile. 'We just might get to a little cooking ourselves after dinner is over. Would that be acceptable to you, Mr Kid Buttercup, sir?'

'Methuselah's ghost!' roared Buttercup. 'You jist dangblasted better believe it, you sweet gal! It ain't often that two folks as good-lookin' as you an' me git the chance to, uh, well, ah – do a little cookin' together. So I'll be seein' you tomorrow evenin' then, honey.'

As he turned to leave the petite schoolmarm, she interrupted his daydreams with a question.

'Excuse me, Mr Buttercup,' she said softly and in an off-hand manner. 'Just how goes your investigation into that nasty bank robbery?'

'Why, I'll have the whole dang thing wrapped up in no time a'tall, Miss Dorsett,' blustered the deputy. 'Ain't nothin' to it. Fact, I'm gonna be ridin' out to the Box CW in jist a little while to see iffen I can put the finishin' touches on all my detective work. You mark my words, darlin' – I'll have them murderin' thieves behind bars by the end of the week. Don't you worry your purty little head over it for another minute.'

'Oh, Mr Buttercup!' The young woman fluttered long eyelashes at him and smiled boldly. 'I do feel so much better having a big, strong lawman such as yourself around to keep a girl safe from harm.'

'Ain't I wonderful?' The Kid's laugh filled the street as he stalked off toward the livery stable, while Martha Dorsett resumed walking in the direction of the small schoolhouse further down the street.

It felt good to be back in the saddle again.

Kid Buttercup was a range-riding drifter by nature and not really given to small-town life. Sitting atop the ragged Petunia, he felt truly at home.

Man and horse kept a steady, if not rapid, pace in the direction of the Box CW Ranch. It was late morning, the sun was high and a cool breeze made for pleasant riding conditions. Sage and yucca dotted arid plains that seemed to spread out forever. Occasional outcroppings of red rock broke the monotony of the flat prairie, but there was little else except blue, open sky to keep the solitary rider company along the well-marked trail leading to the area's largest ranch.

He felt the sharp, stinging pain in his left shoulder before he heard the sound of the rifle. The bullet had only grazed him, but it was followed by a half-dozen others, each of them set on causing him a lot more damage than that. One clipped a notch of flesh from his thigh while another cracked past his ear, far too close for comfort. He caught sight of his attackers crouched low behind a rugged clump of rocks some 200 or more yards distant, and looked frantically about for shelter of his own.

He was rewarded by the shallow remains of an old buffalo wallow twenty-five yards ahead. As another bullet whipped his hat away and another one still tore fringe from his buckskin shirt, the big man reined in hard, then leapt from the saddle and threw himself into the small depression. Quickly he scrambled to take cover while Petunia trotted off to stand docilely in the distance.

Kid Buttercup lay still for a moment, holding tightly to the Winchester he'd pulled from the saddle scabbard before jumping from the back of his horse. He let his cheek rest against the smooth wood of the stock while his eyes focused on the small cluster of rock that thrust up at him from the distance.

Sooner or later they would have to come

looking for him. It all depended on how young, cocky and foolish these boys were … but even so, it was only a matter of time, *whoever* they were.

After only a few short minutes, two figures stood up from the boulders. Both were dead within moments of their backward sprawl to the rocky earth. Buttercup fired five rounds in rapid succession. Two each smacked heavily into the chests of the men who had thought him dead or seriously wounded, while the fifth clipped the shoulder of yet another man who had exposed that small portion of his body to the accurate rifle fire of the wary old range-rider.

'That'll take some o' the starch outa their drawers!' the Kid predicted with a tight grin. 'Let's jist see what kind of stomach they got fer a little more o' *that* action!'

Apparently the bushwhackers had *no* stomach for an open fight. After a hot time of flying lead directed at the man in the buffalo wallow, horses could be heard rapidly departing the scene of the brief skirmish.

Kid Buttercup remained hidden where he was for more than an hour, then ventured out with only the greatest caution.

'Damn cowards!' he swore. 'My pappy taught me not to start somethin' I couldn't finish.' He whistled loudly. Petunia perked up her ears, then trotted over to where her travelling companion stood waiting for her. The big man mounted easily, muttering as he did so, 'Ambushin' is gettin' to be a regular habit around these parts. An' I'll tell you somethin', Petunia, I ain't too happy about it.'

Touching heels to the animal's sides, he rode over to survey the bushwhackers' rocky hiding place, but found nothing of interest. The two he had killed had been taken away so that, other than a confusion of horse-tracks and a couple of splashes of blood, there was nothing to indicate who had been behind the attack. As best he could, Buttercup cleaned his own shallow wounds, then bound them tightly before proceeding on to the Box CW ranch-house, which lay a thirty-minute ride further along the trail.

As he rode into the ranchyard, the Kid quickly saw what Easterly and Crenshaw had commented on earlier. The buildings and grounds were standard ranch-house, large bunkhouse, barn and corral. Nothing unusual in that. No – it was the half-dozen rough-looking cowboys simply sitting around outside of the bunkhouse playing cards drinking and generally passing idle time that stirred the Kid's interest.

From Buttercup's own irregular stints as a cowpuncher, he knew that no rancher liked to have idle hands about in the middle of the day, nor did most cowboys carry pistols during working hours. Scratching absently at the grey-flecked stubble on his chin, the Kid could not help but wonder what the business of the Box CW might really be. He pulled up in front of the big ranch house where Carl Winslow and Jay Tippet lounged in the shade of the front porch.

'Howdy, gents,' the big drifter greeted amiably as he reined down. Winslow and

Tippet quickly rose to their feet, obviously puzzled by the newcomer's ear-to-ear grin. They eyed the bloodstains on his clothing with open curiosity.

'You look like you've had a bit of trouble, lawdog,' Winslow observed casually. 'Anything we can do to help you out?'

'Not likely,' responded Buttercup. The toothy smile remained fixed across his battered countenance.

'Well then, just what *can* we do for you, Deputy?' the handsome rancher asked. Kid Buttercup noted that Tippet remained slightly behind and to the right of his employer, with his hands ever near the grips of those .38 revolvers. 'You lost or something? I mean, the Box CW *is* a pretty far piece from town.'

'I come out to ask you gents a question or two,' the Kid replied. 'But I think I already got all the answers I need about you an' the Box CW.'

'I don't follow you, starpacker.' The rancher's eyes narrowed and his expression turned more serious. 'If you got something to say, then come out with it. We didn't invite you out here and we don't have time for your riddle games.'

'Oh, I think you know *exactly* what I got on my mind, Mr Winslow.' The deputy never let his eyes drift from the two figures before him. 'I really do believe we understand each other jist fine, ol' hoss.'

'Just what's that supposed to mean, trail-trash?' Winslow was goading the big man, but the Kid simply continued to grin in response.

'It means you an' your lap-dog there,' he nodded toward Tippet, 'are runnin' some kinda shady outfit here. Now ol' Jack Crenshaw – who might jist be a better lawman that you give him credit for – he'd tell me that I can't do nothin' without proof. But I'll tell you this much, Mr Big Texas Rancher – iffen this here is an honest cow outfit, then I'm a low-down sheep-herder.'

'If you've got accusations to make, then–' began Winslow.

Buttercup cut him off. 'Hell's bells on a bobcat, Winslow!' he said with a laugh. 'I ain't makin' no kinda accusations. Why, that's the furtherest thang from my feeble brain, ol' pard. You an' your boy there are shore 'nuff innocent as Sunday schoolteachers, 'fer as I know. Howsomever,' he paused a moment to offer up an exaggerated wink, 'I know a skunk when I smell one.'

'You son of a–'

The rancher's curse was cut short as Jay Tippet stepped up a pace while his fingers gripped the butts of the revolvers at his hips. The gunman had heard enough to convince him that they were better off with this meddling drifter dead.

Instantly Buttercup's .44 was trained on Winslow's chest. 'Call your dog off, sonny,' he whispered. The grin never left the battered, rugged face, but the brown eyes were deadly.

'Keep your hands away from your guns, Jay,' the rancher warned the man at his side. 'I don't think this is the time *or* the place for us to deal with Deputy Buttercup.'

'You'd be right about that, Winslow.' The Kid noticed that the hands over at the bunkhouse were starting to pay attention to the scene unfolding before the rancher's home. 'Hmm. Mayhaps I ought to remind you that Marshal Crenshaw an' Joshua Easterly both know where I was headin' this fine mornin', an' I'm certain both of 'em can read sign good enough to see that I got here. So don't do nothin' so stupid as to bring this here thang to violence right in your own front yard. Now, I didn't get these grey hairs by bein' near so dumb as you take me to be, so let me make myself clear oncet an' for all. I'll find out what's goin' on around here, you can be sure o' that. An' when I *do* git it all straight, we can settle our accounts. Me, you an' that little runt of a killer you keep on sich a short leash. Oh, an' keep your bushwhackers at home, Winslow, else you is jist likely to lose a couple *more* men. So long, boys.'

Buttercup kicked Petunia in the ribs, and

the horse wheeled about to race from the ranchyard at a pace none could have expected from such a shabby animal. Within minutes, the deputy was no more than a cloud of dust on the horizon.

'I'll *kill* him,' Tippet snarled to his employer.

'I'd leave him alone was I you, Jay.'

'I'll *kill* him!' Tippet repeated softly, then turned on a heel to disappear into the shadows of the house. As the door slammed behind the man, Carl Winslow was already settling back in his seat with a thoughtful expression on his face.

SIX

Kid Buttercup returned to town late in the afternoon. Briefly, he described the events of the day to Marshal Crenshaw, cleaned and bandaged his own minor wounds, then ate double helpings of steak and fried potatoes at the Good Food Café. After half a dozen assorted rounds of whiskey and beer at the Emerald Palace, the big deputy scratched absently beneath an arm, then made clear his intentions of turning in early for the evening.

'I'm due a good night's sleep, Gerry, old hoss,' he remarked, draining his mug of foamy, golden brew. 'I been shot at, threatened an' dern near killed or worse over the past day or so. This lawdog work is a heap more'n I bargained fer, *amigo*. Anyhow, I'm hittin' the hay early an' I hope I ain't up again afore the sun.'

'If you can keep yourself clear o' trouble long enough to get to that couch in the law office, then good luck to you … Elwood,' O'Cooners commented with a sly gin. With a wince, the Kid pushed away from the bar and headed for the front door of the small saloon. 'Sleep well, bucko. You've plenty o' shenanigans to be unravelling come early mornin'.'

'Sure, sure,' muttered Buttercup as he waved a hand to the red-headed Irishman. 'I'll sleep like a baby.'

'An' could you be after tellin' me a baby *what?*' queried O'Cooners in jest. There was no response from the deputy except that of the batwings swishing behind him as he stepped out into the dark main street of Spit Junction.

'Flower,' a voice rumbled low and deep from the darkness beside the door.

Buttercup pulled his .44 from its holster and lightly shifted his stance to meet any challenge from this unexpected visitor in the night. 'Who the hell is that?' he asked while his eyes adjusted to the faint yellow light that spilled out of the Emerald Palace's dirty windows.

All he could make out was a huge, hulking mountain of shape some five feet away. 'Whoever you be, I got a pistol lined up with your belly, so speak out or git blown to Hell an' the Devil himself. Your choice, bush-whacker!'

'No bushwhacker,' the rumbling voice resumed. 'Otto Wendt.'

It was obvious that the giant was making every effort to speak quietly, but the resulting sounds were something of a mixture of growls and roars. In spite of this, his heavy German accent and enormous size made his identity readily apparent. 'You the flower man?'

'The name's Kid Buttercup,' the Kid replied. He kept the pistol pointed toward the shadowy bulk. 'An' I've a mind to put a few holes through your mangy hide jist on general principles, Otto, ol' pard. What are you doin' waitin' around out here in the dark? You tryin' to finish the ruckus we started the other day over at the Silver Slipper?'

'No. Otto just want to talk, flower man.'

The deputy's vision had adapted to the darkness enough so that he could make out a broad smile on the big bouncer's face.

'How you feel?' asked Otto.

'OK – no thanks to you,' replied Buttercup.

Wendt continued with a grin. 'You leave Mr Burdine alone and Otto leave *you* alone.'

'So that's it,' growled the Kid. 'You think you can waltz over here an' threaten me off your boss-man. Burdine sent you over here thinkin' you could jist–'

'No,' Otto interrupted with no malice to his voice. 'No one send me to see you, flower man. I come to see you because you wrong about Mr Burdine. I come to tell you to watch out for Winslow. People think Otto is dumb just because he not say much, just because his American words are not so good

128

when he talks. But Otto not stupid. Otto hears things. You be careful, flower man. Winslow and Tippet are bad men, but you are wrong about Mr Burdine.'

'I'll be sheep-dipped,' Buttercup exclaimed as he holstered the big revolver. 'Thanks fer the words there, Otto, but jist why do you think this Burdine feller is OK? He strikes me as an ornery cuss. You really an' fer true think he ain't behind this bank robbery business?'

'Mr Burdine *help* Otto,' the giant rumbled as softly as he could manage. 'When wife and baby sick, Mr Burdine bring doctor, medicine, food. Mr Burdine give Otto good job in his saloon. He is not bank robber, flower man. You look somewhere else for robbers and killers. You maybe look for them at Box CW Ranch.'

'I'll think on that one, Otto, old hoss,' the Kid replied, then stuck his hand out toward the bouncer. 'You can jist bet your shiny bald head I'll sleep on it, pard.'

'Good,' Otto announced, his wide smile

showing bright white teeth in the light from the saloon windows. The two men grasped hands in a firm grip that threatened to crunch bones in the deputy's hand. Otto released his hold whilst saying, 'I go back to work now, flower man.'

'Goodnight, *amigo*.' Buttercup shook the throbbing hand as he turned away from Wendt. Each went his separate way into the dark night.

'Crazy, mixed-up twists an' turns every time I look up,' muttered the drifter as he stalked off toward the law office. 'Iffen I had any sense a'tall, I'd head straight fer dear Petunia an' haul my carcass right out of town.'

But even as he spoke the words, he knew he would stay. Already turning the events of the past few days over in his mind, the big man trudged on to the marshal's head-quarters and a restless night on the frayed, sagging couch.

Kid Buttercup was up early next morning.

He washed before heading out for a big breakfast at the Good Food Café, then made his rounds of the town, asking questions about Ned Burdine, Otto Wendt, Carl Winslow, Jay Tippet and anyone else who came to mind. By late morning he was dry, hungry and filled with the random information he'd collected by way of his informal investigation. He stopped by the hardware store to see if Joshua Easterly might care to join him for a drink.

'Too old to be hittin' the bottle this early in the mornin',' Kid,' Easterly joked lightly in reply. 'Howsomever, I'll be happy to grab a bite to eat over at the Emerald Palace while you have a shot or two, if you like. I got to eat lunch soon, anyway.'

'Then shut down the shop so's we can get a-movin',' roared Buttercup enthusiastically. 'I'm as dry as a desert an' purt' near twice as dusty.'

Easterly hung a 'Back Soon' sign on his door as they left the store. The two men began their short walk toward the little tavern, but noticed the local schoolmarm coming their way down the same side of Main Street.

'Waahoo, doggies,' grinned the Kid. 'There's the purty little thang that jist might make this here stopover in Spit Junction worth my while.'

'Mind your manners, Buttercup,' warned Easterly in a stern tone. 'She's a lady.'

'Hell's bells on a babcat!' roared the deputy. 'I know what she is, old hoss.'

'You don't seem to act like it.'

'You're jist jealous, you old goat. That little lady's done taken quite a shine to me fer shore.' He winked at the silver haired gunman who walked beside him. 'Besides, I got me a dinner date an' you don't.'

Easterly's glance at him was sharp. 'What did you say?' he hissed. 'You got a dinner date with Miss *Dorsett?*'

'You heard me, granpappy,' Buttercup replied with a smirk.

Martha Dorsett's approach prevented any further conversation between the two companions. 'Hello, gentlemen,' the petite young woman said in a soft, cultured voice that almost seemed to purr. Her smile was warm and sincere. 'We have such a perfect fall day today, don't you agree?'

'Yes ma'am,' agreed the hardware store owner. 'These days 'tween summer heat an' winter freeze are as good as it gets here in the Panhandle.'

'Shore 'nuff,' added Buttercup, as a grin began to spread across his battered face. 'Now, Miss Martha honey, I'm eatin' light fer lunch 'cause you promised to fix me a home-cooked meal fer dinner this evenin'. You still gonna cook fer me tonight, ain't you, darlin'?'

'Why of course, Deputy Buttercup,' the young woman replied, favouring the big man with a sweet, innocent smile. 'You just come round my house about six o'clock this evening and I'll have a meal for you that you'll not soon forget.'

'I'll be there fer certain,' the Kid assured her, his grin now threatening to swallow the remainder of his features as the school-teacher quickly said her goodbyes and then continued on toward home for her lunch-break.

'You better be on your best behaviour to-night,' Easterly cautioned as they continued on to the Emerald Palace. 'Heaven help you iffen Jack or me get any bad reports back from that lady.'

'Why, Joshua, ol' pard,' interjected Butter-cup, 'I can guarantee you that Miss Martha will see some of my very best behaviour this evenin' an' that's a puredee fact.'

Easterly sighed heavily. The Kid's answer did not really serve to put his fears to rest, but there was little else he could do to keep the big drifter under control.

Within minutes, the two had taken stools at the far end of the bar. It was early for lunch, so the faded green walls of the Emerald Palace held few customers as yet. After building sandwiches from the lunch tray, they ate a light meal. Easterly had a cup of coffee while Buttercup savoured a double shot of whiskey followed by a tall, cold beer.

As O'Cooners refilled the old shootist's cup with hot coffee and provided another double shot with a second beer for the buckskin-clad deputy, conversation turned to the investigation at hand.

'So,' Easterly began. 'You still think Ned Burdine is the man behind all of this?'

Buttercup scratched absently beneath his arm with one soiled finger before replying. 'Well, I can't rightly say no more.'

'All that shootin' yesterday changed your mind, huh?'

'That's part of it fer shore, but that ain't the whole of the story, Joshua.'

'What're you gettin' at, Kid?' Easterly asked with a puzzled expression. 'Not twenty-four hours since, you was rarin' to hang the whole dang thing on Burdine. What happened?'

'I had me a little talk with Otto Wendt last night.'

'Nobody talks with Otto,' O'Cooners

interrupted, leaning on the counter nearby, 'Hell, that big German don't say nothin' to nobody.'

'He shore as hell talked to me last night,' Buttercup assured his companions earnestly. Briefly, the deputy summarized his conversation with the bouncer, then added, 'This mornin' I've been askin' folks questions about ornery ol' Ned Burdine, Carl Winslow an' others.'

The hardware store man raised an eyebrow, surprised by this show of initiative, and met the Kid's gaze directly. 'You pick up any useful information?'

Buttercup shook his head. 'Not about the bank robbery,' he replied. 'But I found out a few things about Burdine.' He drained his mug of beer and O'Cooners refilled it without having to be asked. 'Did you fellers know that Burdine's got a reputation with the down-an-outs as a man what'll give handouts when needed, an' helps folks when they find 'emselves in trouble?'

'You're crazy, Kid,' chuckled Easterly.

'Somebody's been stringin' you along for a fool.'

The freckled face of Gerry O'Cooners split with a wide grin. 'Sure an' now, they're greenin' you, Elwood me laddie.'

'I'm only tellin' you what I hear.' The Kid sipped slowly from his mug. 'Remember, I don't like the sorry cuss a'tall, but when you ask folks who ain't got much in this town, they'll all tell you who they go to when they need a little help – an' that's Ned Burdine.'

'Ain't that a kick in the head?' the old gunman grinned. 'All we see is a tough-nosed, hard-to-get-along-with businessman, an' there's a whole 'nother side to this critter that we didn't even *know* about.'

'That's the way folks say he wants it.'

Buttercup drained the beer, chased it with another double shot of whiskey that O'Cooners automatically placed before him. 'They all say that Burdine swears 'em to secrecy. Hell, to hear 'em talk, he's like some kinda guardian angel.'

'Then how come they're tellin' you his

secret now?' asked the still-sceptical O'Cooners. 'Why should they give him away to an ugly stranger the likes of you?'

''Cause they heard I suspected him of that bank robbery an' they wanted to change my mind about ol' Saint Ned,' the Kid responded briefly.

'I suppose it *could* be true,' allowed Easterly. 'But it's a damn strange turn of events, an' that's a fact.'

O'Cooners took a pause in the conversation to alter the direction of their discussion. 'So, if you let Burdine off your hook, then just who would you be blamin' for the bank robbery, Mr Kirklymoore?'

'And for the attack on you yesterday?' added Easterly as the Kid winced painfully. He paused a moment, then framed another question for his companion. 'Just who knew you were riding out to the Box CW yesterday morning?'

'There really weren't many folks that knew 'bout that,' the Kid growled. 'I was all fer layin' that ambush at Burdine's door afore my talk with Otto las' night. Now, I ain't got much notion *who* to blame. Blast it all, outside o' you, Jack an' the boy at the livery stable, the only person I talked with yesterday mornin' was that purty little gal, Miss Martha.'

O'Cooners grinned and winked at his companions. 'She's the one, to be sure, me buckos.'

'Go to hell, Irishman!' boomed the deputy, but he followed the explosion with equally enthusiastic laughter.

The old hardware store man beside him simply sipped his coffee in studied silence.

'I'm fer certain the Box CW is mixed up in all this somehow or other,' confided Buttercup, sobering again. 'They's altogether too many idle hardcases out there fer them to be an honest cow outfit. They's up to some kinda no good, an' that's a fact!'

'That's what you said about Burdine yesterday,' Easterly reminded him. 'Now you tell us he's in line for bishop or some such thing as that. 'Sides, if it was the Box

CW that set up that little ambush, then how did they get word you was comin' out that way? You got your suspicions, but you don't have any proof, Kid. That's been your problem all along. But you can't go around accusin' folks of robbin' banks without some kinda evidence.'

The big man banged a fist upon the table top. 'But you shoulda seen them cowboys sittin' around that yard there, playin' cards an' sich as that. Ever' single dagblasted one of 'em was packin' iron an' loaded fer bear. Don't tell me that's a hard-workin' cow ranch. No siree, bobcats! That Carl Winslow is up to some shady foolishness, an' further-more–' he paused to drain the big mug he held in a dirty paw – 'that Jay Tippet feller is a cheap gunman if ever I seen one, an',' he eyed Easterly with a knowing grin anima-ting his rough features, 'I've seen a few gunmen in my time, ol' pard.'

The older man met the other's gaze with rock-steady eyes. 'Be that as it may,' he said, 'you simply got to come up with the goods on the Box CW if you want to make it stick. All you're gonna do is drive the outlaws under cover with all your stompin' around.'

'Or flush 'em into the open.' Buttercup's grin was infectious. He winked at Easterly and O'Cooners in turn.

'You might just be right,' Easterly observed quietly.

Soon the conversation made yet another turn as the hardware store owner reminded the barkeep that his bride-to-be should arrive on the stage the day after tomorrow.

'Sure an' now, she'll be here, me fine friend,' O'Cooners replied, hardly able to contain his joy at the prospect. 'All I've worked for these past years is about to come true. Indeed, 'tis sure to be one of the finest days o' me life.'

'No doubt about it,' echoed the older man.

'Ha!' mocked Kid Buttercup, who was never one to stay quiet for long. 'If you're smart, you'll sell this place an' leave town afore she gits here. Ain't no woman gonna cross an ocean, then a continent, jist to trap a man inta marriage, not lessen no one'd have her back there in good ol' Ireland.'

'Leave off, Buttercup,' the bartender growled in an ominous tone. 'I'll see iffen I can't straighten out that nose of yourn for you if you don't keep it out o' my business.'

'Can't you stay out of trouble for more than a few minutes at a time, son?' Easterly asked, shaking his head at the drifter's natural inclination toward violent conflict. 'I can't imagine how you've lived this long if you make a habit out of insultin' other men's wives an' womenfolk.'

'I ain't insultin' nobody,' replied the temporary lawman, obviously aggrieved. 'I'm jist statin' the facts an' tryin' to git this poor Irish jackass to listen to reason. He's still got time to save hisself afore it's too late, if only he'll be guided by ol' Buttercup.'

'We're leavin', Gerry,' announced Easterly as he grabbed the big man by a buckskin-clad arm and tugged him toward the doorway at a rapid pace.

'Good day to you, Joshua,' called the barkeep. 'An' good *riddance* to your pet gorilla.'

'I ain't makin' any claim to him,' responded the gunman as he shoved Buttercup through the door and right into the path of Jack Crenshaw. The marshal had been about to enter the faded drinking parlour as the Kid came out in a rush. Easterly followed close behind.

'Whoa hoss.' Crenshaw put his hands out to halt the deputy's stumbling progress. Joshua Easterly joined the pair before the saloon. 'You two in a hurry?' Crenshaw asked.

'Just movin' Buttercup along before O'Cooners decides to make lunch-meat out of him.'

'Why, was that Irish 'tater to try sich a thing, I'd take hold of him an'–'

'This big ape still ridin' the Irish about his girl?' asked the marshal with a frown.

'Yep,' nodded Easterly. 'Seems he just can't stay out of trouble to save his worthless soul.'

'I got things to do this afternoon, anyway,' the deputy grinned. 'I'm gonna get me a hot bath an' shave, an'–'

'That'll certainly help,' commented Crenshaw. 'What's the occasion? Birthday, maybe?'

'He's havin' a meal at Miss Martha's tonight,' explained Easterly.

'Stand back, boys,' the shabby, battered figure in buckskins announced with a flourish of dramatic gestures. 'Kid Buttercup's a-goin' sparkin' tonight!'

SEVEN

Martha Dorsett had prepared a meal fit for a king. Chicken, dumplings and light, fluffy biscuits filled the big deputy to bursting. Two large wedges of apple pie provided a happy ending to one of the Kid's finest dinners in recent memory. He floated on a cloud of contentment as he pushed away from the tiny table in the cosy kitchen where they had eaten the evening feast.

'Shall we step into the parlour, Deputy Buttercup?' The young woman's invitation was both sweet and promising. Her companion followed in a fashion of a large, but not especially bright, mongrel pup.

Within moments, the two were in the parlour with china coffee cups in hand. Sitting beside the lady upon a delicate love-seat, the roughly-dressed giant felt out of place. He sipped his coffee with as little noise as possible, all the while trying not to stare at the hint of cleavage that showed above the neckline of the schoolmarm's satin gown. Moving his eyes about the room, the Kid surveyed the modest surroundings while the young woman talked briefly of her move to Spit Junction.

'It really did seem to be a good decision for me at the time,' she confided. She spoke in her most pleasant voice as she described her graduation from school back East, the death of her parents and her search for employment. Without hesitation, she launched into her experiences in the Texas Panhandle. 'Teaching here in this rugged region has been quite an experience, I can assure you, Deputy Buttercup.'

The Kid listened to the tone, but not to the words. He noticed the dancing orange flames in the tiny fireplace, the few articles of furniture that decorated the small parlour along with the thick oriental carpet covering the plank floor. The schoolmarm's little house consisted only of an entrance hall, kitchen, parlour and, he surmised, a bedroom at the back of the house.

Perhaps, the drifter grinned slyly, he might get to see that room later in the evening.

He tried to return his attention to the lady's words as they continued to spill forth in reckless abandon, but his struggle was in vain. When Kid Buttercup had to choose between conversation and cleavage, well ... cleavage won every time.

'So, all seemed reasonably well with my new situation – until recently,' she concluded with a sigh that did wonders for that part of her anatomy that Buttercup found so compelling. 'Now, I just don't know whom to turn to, Mr Kid Buttercup. I only know that I feel safe and secure knowing that you are now on the job.'

'I'm jist happy to be of service, honey,' the Kid replied gallantly, his smile stretching from ear to ear. 'You need anythin' at all, you jist call on ol' Kid Buttercup. There ain't nothin' to be afraid of while I'm on the job.'

'Well, I certainly hope we can count on you to find the awful men who killed poor old Mr Philbertt and robbed our bank. Why, merciful heavens, with those ruffians on the loose, there's not one of us decent citizens safe to walk the streets of this town.'

'I'll be wrappin' this thang up in no time, darlin',' bragged Buttercup as he slipped an arm around his companion. 'I've got the whole thang figured out. All I got to do is put together a few final pieces of evidence an' then we'll throw the whole kit'n kaboodle of 'em into the jailhouse.'

'Can you tell me the identities of these terrible beasts?' the young woman asked with a slight shiver before she snuggled closer to the big buckskin-clad figure seated beside her. 'I want to stay clear of any potential danger.'

'Of course you do, Miss Martha,' Buttercup agreed comfortingly. 'You jist keep yourself away from that sorry scoundrel Carl Winslow an' his hardcase outfit at the Box CW. They's the ones behind all the trouble around these parts, but don't you worry about it fer another minute. They ain't gonna git away from me, an' that's a fact fer certain.'

The schoolteacher tilted her head to gaze into the Kid's face with unconcealed admiration. 'I am simply fascinated by your deductions, Deputy Buttercup,' she whispered. 'How did you arrive at these conclusions so swiftly?'

'Well, my little prairie flower, it really ain't no secret,' Buttercup gushed. 'All this trouble started up about the time Winslow moved into this territory, an' some of them Box CW boys was in town the night of the robbery. 'Fact, a couple of them fellers was seen on the street late that night with a, uh, well, a soiled dove from over to the Silver Slipper. Anyway, on top of all that, I was shot at while ridin' out to the Box CW. There jist ain't no doubt in my mind that Winslow an' Tippet is the mangy coyotes who robbed that bank an' killed Philbertt.'

'And poor, dear Mr Philbertt locked in his

vault – and dressed up like a woman!' The lady shuddered delicately. 'I simply cannot imagine what things are coming to when crimes such as this can happen.'

'Well, don't fret, honey. Like I say, I'll have them varmints behind bars quick as a wink.' And just to demonstrate how quick that would be, he *did* wink.

'I suppose that Marshal Crenshaw is equally alert in this matter? That is, you can count on him for his complete support in apprehending these horrible bandits, can't you?'

'I ain't so shore I can count on *anybody*, sugar-babe. I seem to be the only feller hereabouts what can see things as they really are. Your local law jist don't have the gumption to git in there an' mix things up. You know, stir the pot an' make somethin' happen. 'That's why ol' Kid Buttercup is gonna have to be the man what prods these nasty critters out into the open. I'll git 'em, though, honey. You jist wait an' see.'

'Oh, I'm sure you will,' Martha replied,

resting her head upon his chest. 'I'm just *sure* you will.'

'What are you so interested in all this foolishness for, anyhow, honey-bunch?' queried the Kid as he buried his nose in her soft, red hair to breathe deeply of her floral scent.

'Just a woman's natural curiosity,' responded the young schoolmarm, as her fingers began to trace patterns along his flat, muscled stomach. 'Besides, my life here is so quiet and dull that all this excitement just makes me feel tingly all over.'

The big man grinned hugely. 'I know just what you mean,' he agreed. 'I feel kinda tingly myself, right now.'

Suddenly, Martha Dorsett was on her feet. 'Well, the hour is growing late, Deputy Buttercup. I have enjoyed our visit, but I do have school early in the morning. You will excuse me for the evening, won't you?'

'But ... I thought ... well, maybe we could...' the deputy fumbled, searching vainly for the right words. Before he could find them, the petite schoolmistress pulled him to his feet and then gently urged him toward the front door.

Reaching the oak portal, the young woman turned the Kid about quickly so that they were facing one another again. Lifting up on her tip-toes, she pulled his head down so that their lips could meet in a passionate kiss. Finally releasing him, she opened the door before speaking.

'I promise you something better than apple pie for dessert if you'll come back on Friday evening.'

Their eyes met, and what the Kid saw in her frank stare set his mind racing with possibilities. 'Good night, Deputy Buttercup,' she whispered.

Just before the door closed softly, the big drifter managed a hoarse response. He didn't think the woman heard it, and frankly was in too much of romantic daze to really care. Dreamy-eyed, he turned to walk back in the direction of the town's centre.

They jumped him just as he stepped off

the porch.

There were three of them, but even then they probably would have stood little chance except that one landed a blow to the Kid's head right at the start. While his hat cushioned most of the impact, the shock was enough to make the giant go weak in the knees while the three owlhoots swarmed over him in a frenzy of punches and kicks.

Kid Buttercup's right fist exploded in one man's face, leaving nothing but a bloody blur where features had existed moments before. The man stumbled backward, then sat down hard with crimson dripping from almost every hole in his head – including a few that had not existed prior to this evening's assault.

A second hardcase had his arm wrenched from its socket, but still managed a sharp kick, that caught the deputy square in the belly. Letting out a whoosh of air, the Kid released the man's arm only to be socked again from behind with the same hard object as before.

Dazed, Buttercup turned upon this menace, only to find a tall, rangy man wielding an axe handle firmly in his grip. Quicker than anyone could have expected, the drifter kicked the man hard between the legs, then snatched the wooden axe handle from his fingers. With the clubbing weapon now in his own grasp, Buttercup managed a swift, savage blow toward his attacker that landed with a heavy thud on the rangy individual's shoulder. Swallowing a grunt of pain, Rangy was knocked to earth while the deputy twisted around to account for his other assailant.

He was only a moment too late.

A left and right rocked Buttercup's head and split his lips. His own big right hand sprang out to connect with a nose that spurted a stream of scarlet into the dark night. Seizing this momentary advantage, the battered lawman became a human battering-ram, launching blow after blow until his opponents crumbled into a senseless heap at his feet.

Shaking his head to clear the red haze of pain and confusion, the Kid announced to the dark of night, 'That should end *that* little ruckus.'

'Not quite,' a voice replied from behind.

This time a gun-barrel found a spot just behind the big man's ear that sent the ground rushing up to meet him and made the world go blacker than the night.

Kid Buttercup was down and out, a mountain of bruised, bleeding flesh measuing his not inconsiderable length on the cold, hard ground. There had been a fourth man present who had stayed out of the fight until the bitter end. It was this fourth man who now pushed a Colt .38 pistol back into a holster and then proceeded to motivate the battered Box CW hands who lay sprawled in a small circle around the fallen deputy.

Jay Tippet nudged one of the men with a boot-toe. 'Get up. We've got to get this bastard hogtied and out of sight.'

The figure groaned, then struggled to sit erect. 'Move it,' snarled the little gunman in hushed tones. 'The boss said to haul him out to headquarters and sit on him. Now, get up and *move!*'

Slowly the three men came to life. They carried out their instructions to dragging the Kid out of sight behind the teacher's house and then binding him securely before loading him on to a horse. Within minutes the men were quietly slipping from town in the direction of the Box CW Ranch.

Late morning found Joshua Easterly walking the streets of Spit Junction in search of Kid Buttercup.

By now he'd expected to hear from the deputy. Indeed, he'd been fully expecting the Kid to come thumping on his door at first light, set on giving him a blow-by-blow account of the previous evening's dinner date.

But the big man was nowhere to be found, and when Easterly checked, he found

Petunia, the Kid's ragged horse, quietly chomping grain at the livery stable. When he made further enquiries, it transpired that neither O'Cooners nor Crenshaw had seen the rugged drifter either.

Shaking his head perplexedly, Easterly found himself walking quickly in the direction of the schoolteacher's home on the outskirts of town. He had a hunch the Kid's absence was no accident – and it was a hunch he intended to follow through to a conclusion.

The tiny box of a home stood dark and silent this morning. Easterly knew that Martha Dorsett would be at the school-house at this time of day, but still he climbed the few steps to the wooden porch, then knocked at the front door on the chance that the Kid might be inside. While he could not imagine how the drifter could have made that much progress in the schoolmarm's affections in just one evening, he supposed it to be a good idea to give yet another series of knocks just in case the brash Buttercup had managed to spend the night at Miss Martha's residence.

When no reply came from the house, Easterly turned to step down from the porch. For just a moment, a ray of sunlight splashed on an object in the bushes. Frowning, the old shootist moved around to the side of the porch to investigate further, then crouched low in order to look through some brush that had grown up on the right-hand side of the plank platform that fronted the teacher's house.

'What in tarnation...?'

The silver-haired gunman reached a hand into the bushes. His fingers closed around the object and he withdrew his arm from the tangle of prickly brush. Softly he mumbled, 'That hunch o' mine is itchin' at me.'

Standing, Easterly opened his clenched fist to reveal a metal star. It was a deputy badge, and it looked an awful lot like the one that had so recently been given to the Kid.

Stuffing the piece of tin into his pocket, the hardware store owner took long, purposeful strides toward the marshal's office.

'Jack!' Easterly called as he stepped through the doorway of the law office little more than a minute later. 'Hey, Jack!'

'Hold on a damn' minute!' Marshal Crenshaw called from the cellblock out back. 'I'm comin' as quick as I can, dagblast it!'

'I think somethin's happened to the Kid,' observed the gunman as Crenshaw stepped out into the cluttered office. Easterly pulled the badge from his pocket and tossed it on the lawman's desk. 'I found this in the bushes beside Martha Dorsett's porch. We know Buttercup was out there las' night, an' ain't nobody seen him all mornin'. There's somethin' wrong, Jack. I got a powerful hunch ol' Buttercup's in big trouble.'

'Hell, I doubt it, Joshua,' Crenshaw replied as he slumped into a chair behind his desk. 'Just 'cause you find a badge in the brush don't mean there's anythin' wrong. He could of dropped the dang thing, or it might not even be his. For all we know, the Kid just up an' decided to leave town. He weren't exactly enthusiastic about this job to begin with, you know.'

'His horse is still down at the livery, Jack.'

'He might have stole a better one,' grinned the marshal. 'From what I seen of that horse of his, he'd be better off with just about any nag he could pick around town.'

'This ain't funny,' Easterly cautioned grimly. His sky-blue eyes turned icy for a moment, before softening again. 'I think we ought to at least talk with Miss Martha,' suggested the gunman.

'What, an' ask her if Kid Buttercup spent the *night* with her?' Crenshaw suggested with heavy sarcasm.

Easterly ignored that and said instead, 'We could at least ask her if she knows anythin' about what the Kid had planned for today.'

'Well,' the starpacker agreed, 'she *was* supposed to have dinner with him las' night, so maybe she *does* have some idea where he's at. I don't think you got anythin' to be worryin' about, Joshua, but if it'll set your mind at ease, well – let's go ask her a few questions.'

'Just humour me,' grumbled Easterly.

'Miss Martha should be breakin' for lunch about now,' the lawman opined, tugging his hat down as the cool fall breeze brushed against him. 'Howsomever,' he added, as a sly grin pulled at the corners of his mouth, 'there's somethin' here I don't really understand.'

'What's that?' asked the older man, his long strides still carrying him quickly in the direction of the small meeting-house that served as the town's school, church and general gathering spot.

'If I recall correctly, then you weren't gonna have no part in this here investigation,' Crenshaw said with a soft laugh. 'You told me that you weren't no detective, an' you weren't no lawman either. You said I was on my *own*.'

'That's right, Jack.'

'Then what were you doin' out this mornin', pokin' around Martha Dorsett's house an' snoopin' after that big, ugly Buttercup?'

'I suppose I'm jus' too damn' nosy for my own good,' replied Easterly with a smile of his own. But his expression quickly sobered, because he was very genuinely worried. 'Besides, it was me that got Buttercup into this mess in the first place. Now hurry up so's we can find out what's goin' *on* around here.'

'Right with you, Joshua.'

As they approached the building, they could see a small group of children dispersing into the surrounding houses and buildings while the schoolteacher closed the door behind her. Martha Dorsett turned toward her home, but noticed the rapid approach of the local lawman and his friend from the hardware store down Main Street.

'Hello, Marshal,' the pretty schoolmarm greeted warmly, adding a nod of acknowledgement, 'Mr Easterly.'

'Mornin' ma'am,' said Crenshaw, and

each of them returned her smile in spite of the official nature of their visit.

'Is there something I can do for you gentlemen?'

'Yes, ma'am,' Crenshaw began. 'You see, Miss Martha, we been lookin' for my deputy, but no one seems to've seen him all mornin' long. We were hopin' you might be able to point us in the right direction.'

'Well, I'm afraid you will have to add me to the list of those who have not seen Deputy Buttercup today. I've been teaching the children since early in the day, so have not had the opportunity to encounter your assistant as yet.'

'Yes ma'am,' Crenshaw replied. 'But what about las' night? Was he over to your house for dinner yesterday evening?'

'Yes, of course,' answered the school-teacher, with crimson creeping into her cheeks. 'But I hardly see how my personal life could be of any concern to the law. I can assure you that Deputy Buttercup and I have maintained a proper social distance in all our...'

'Certainly, Miss Martha.' The marshal hurriedly raised his hands to silence the woman. 'I had no intention of pryin' into your social life, an' I sure as heck wasn't implyin' no ... well ... *impropriety*. I was only tryin' to find out just where the Kid was las' night, an' if he said anythin' that might tell us what he had in mind for today. Do you have any idea where he might be?'

'No. We had dinner, and then a brief, pleasant conversation. After that he left my house to return to his sleeping quarters at the law office.'

Without warning, Crenshaw snapped his fingers and let loose an exclamation of surprise that brought another blush to Martha Dorsett's cheeks. 'Uh, pardon me, Miss Martha,' he excused. 'But that reminds me o' somethin'. He never slept at the jailhouse las' night!' The starpacker made his announcement while staring into his companion's sky-blue eyes. 'I hadn't thought about that, but now that I think on it, the blanket he'd been usin' was all folded up on top of the file cabinet. He ain't been back to the office since he left there for Miss Martha's place.'

'Ma'am.' Easterly now entered the conversation. 'Are you *certain* the Kid didn't say anythin' that could give us a clue where he might've gone today? Anythin' at all that might indicate what he had planned?'

'He mentioned something about bringing those disreputable bank robbers to justice,' the schoolmarm replied after a moment's thought. 'But I really couldn't say what Deputy Buttercup's plans were, Mr Easterly. He did not confide in me.'

Easterly's eyes took on a hard, cold aspect as he searched the woman's face. They looked into one another's eyes for a long moment, before the old man continued, 'Did you hear anythin' unusual las' night, after the Kid left your house?'

'I'm afraid I don't understand what you mean?'

'Just what I asked, ma'am.' The old

shootist made his question sound casual. 'I was only wonderin' if you might've heard any type of strange noises after the deputy left for home yesterday evenin', an'...'

'Marshal,' Martha Dorsett interrupted. 'I really am not able to help you. I had dinner with Deputy Buttercup and that is *all*. Now, if you will excuse me, I simply *must* be going.'

'Yes ma'am,' Marshal Crenshaw replied, hurriedly doffing his hat in an attempt to placate her. 'Sorry to've troubled you, Miss Martha.'

'No trouble, Marshal,' Martha Dorsett said with a smile for the lawman. 'I do hope you find your deputy soon. I have no doubt that there has just been some silly misunderstanding.'

'Yes ma'am. Sorry to've wasted your time.'

'Good day, gentlemen.'

The young woman turned and began to walk home.

Joshua Easterly stood silently, lost in thought. Somewhere between the schoolteacher's house and the marshal's office, Kid Buttercup had disappeared. In a town the size of Spit Junction, that simply did not leave much room in which to search.

EIGHT

Kid Buttercup's head throbbed to the persistent beat of a loudly thumping drum. He quickly identified this pounding as the beat of his own heart. The dry, thick stick in his mouth turned out to be his own tongue, and upon it there sat a nasty taste, as if he'd spent the entire evening kissing a mule.

Slitting his eyes allowed daylight to enter the closed room of his mind. Colourful sparks exploded inside his battered skull, and the pain in his head intensified so rapidly that he thought he was going to lose what little food remained in his stomach. He closed his eyes again and mentally evaluated his situation. Beyond the pain, the Kid was bound hand and foot with rope. Other than this, everything seemed to be just dandy this fine morning.

He examined his surroundings. He had been dumped in the corner of a ramshackle shed. The roughly-built shack showed unpainted walls of weathered wood, with a sagging door at the front, flanked by small windows of dirty, cracked glass on either side. A dirt floor gave the room a damp, musty smell that was enhanced by trash and, lining the walls, broken and discarded ranch equipment. Near the door, two hard-looking men in cowboy garb sat on stools, playing cards on an upturned crate that was positioned between them. One of the hands was thirty-something, with a chunky, powerful frame, dark hair, a week's growth of beard and a badly broken nose. The other hand was tall, broad-shouldered, deep-chested and no more than twenty years of age. Light, sand-coloured hair topped his head and whiskers decorated his upper lip. Both men wore pistols at their hips, and the Kid spied his own gunbelt and revolver stacked beside the door.

Reaching a decision, Buttercup lay as still

as possible and quietly set to work on the ropes binding his hands behind his back. He quickly discovered that the knots had been tied either carelessly, hurriedly or both. Tying a limp figure in the dark is not a simple task, so he began to carefully explore his bonds for any hint of slack or clumsy knots. Continuing to feign unconsciousness, it was a matter of minutes before the ropes were loose enough to slip his hands free in readiness as soon as opportunity for escape presented itself. He knew such a chance was bound to come: vigilance is never maintained for long.

His two guards smoked steadily while sipping from a whiskey bottle. Generally, they ignored the big heap that lay quietly in the corner. They had no reason to take notice of Kid Buttercup. After the battle of the previous evening, with the resulting blow to the big man's head, the two hard-case cowboys assumed the deputy would give them no trouble. This was, of course, exactly what the Kid had hoped they would believe. He could afford to be patient.

'What do you suppose the boss is gonna do with that big feller, Chet?' the youngster asked of his chunky companion, taking another small sip from the whiskey bottle.

'Hell, I don't know,' Chet replied while holding his hand out for the bottle. 'More'n likely he'll be dead afore much longer – but I never could figure out what the boss'll do, Sandy.'

'That's a fact,' Sandy grinned, returning his attention to the soiled, crumpled cards he held in his hand.

'After he gets a little life in him, we'll give a holler so's Winslow can have a go at him.' Chet threw a few small coins into a pot with a grin. 'That oughta provide a little sport around here, fer a fact.'

'Yeah,' Sandy shook his head slowly then rubbed a finger across the sparse hairs upon his upper lip. 'I seen Tippet work a feller over with a red-hot runnin' iron one night over in Oklahomy. He had that man singin' real loud afore he was finished.'

Chet chuckled softly as they both cast a quick glance toward the bound figure in the far corner. 'He's gon' have a few nasty surprises when he wakes up, an' that's fer sure. Now,' he raked in the small pot before him then pulled all the cards together to begin his shuffle, 'let's play poker, boy.'

As the two cowhands resumed their card game, Buttercup closed his eyes and tested the loose ropes once more. Yes, he could easily free himself when necessary. Mentally, he congratulated himself. He'd been correct. Carl Winslow was obviously the man behind all the lawlessness in the surrounding countryside. With a mental snort, the Kid thought back to his first encounter with Winslow. The rancher claimed to have had some of his stock rustled. Hogwash! The sumbitch had probably only made that up so's it would appear that he was being hit by the outlaws just like everyone else in the area. And all that talk, demanding to know what the marshal was planning to do to bring the guilty parties to justice! Damn, but that Winslow feller was a hypocrite!

As the sun climbed higher, Crenshaw and Easterly rode toward the Box CW ranch house at a trot. As the marshal had grown to share Easterly's concern for Kid Buttercup, so he'd started asking the silver-haired ex-gunman to tell him everything he knew. Trouble was, Easterly didn't *know* anything, not for sure, though he suspected a whole lot. With a shake of the head, he'd confessed, 'All I got is a couple half-baked ideas, Jack. Nothin' to back 'em up. I could just as easy be right as be wrong. But...'

Tight-lipped, Crenshaw said, 'You just talk, Joshua. I'm a-listenin'.'

Now, two hours later, Crenshaw focused his attention on Carl Winslow and Jay Tippet, as they rose from seats on the front porch and stepped out into the yard before the home and headquarters of the prosperous ranch. Easterly let his eyes drift about the property, taking note of the ranch-hands who lounged in the doorway of the bunkhouse, the placing of the barn, corral and small shed set off behind the other buildings. Briefly, he caught a glimpse of a figure standing at the window of that distant shack. His mind began working at a meaning to go with the furtive face at a cracked, grimy window, and a grim smile played briefly at the corners of his mouth.

'Mornin', Marshal,' Winslow called out. His hands were on his hips, which placed his gun-hand very near to the Colt's pistol he carried high up on his right side. 'What brings you way out here to the Box CW? You decide to look into all that cattle-rustling I've been complaining about?'

'No, Mr Winslow,' Crenshaw replied, reining in so that his horse stood fifteen feet in front of the handsome rancher. 'I told you that's not in my jurisdiction. There ain't nothin' I can do except pass it along to the county sheriff's office.'

Easterly kept his eyes on the little gunman who stood off to the side and behind his boss. He knew that Tippet was a professional. How good he was, he could not know for certain – but the fact that he was still alive spoke for his abilities with the .38 revolvers strapped about his waist. The professional was always the man to watch when trouble seemed likely.

The rancher's face displayed his contempt. 'Seems we've had this talk before, Marshal,' he said. 'If you didn't come out here to help, then what *do* you want, Crenshaw?'

'I'm lookin' for my deputy.'

Winslow laughed loudly. 'Jay and I had a little talk with him once, and I don't recall sending out any more invitations. Just what in hell do you think Big, Ugly and Stupid would be doing out here?'

'That's what *I* want to know, Mr Winslow.' The marshal met the other man's gaze with steady, hard eyes. 'Now, how about you just answer me straight out – have you seen my deputy out this way?'

'As you say, Marshal,' Winslow said, his grin turning ugly. 'You're out of your juris-diction.'

'*I'm* not.'

All eyes turned to Easterly.

'What the hell–' Winslow began, until the old shootist cut him off.

'We're gonna have some answers before we leave here, Winslow. Now, you can talk to the marshal, or you can talk to me. I don't really give a damn, just so long as you *do* talk.' Easterly's voice was soft, cold and determined.'

Winslow suppressed an involuntary shudder. 'What have *you* got to do with any of this, anyway?' he blustered. 'I don't have to listen to a broken-down old storekeeper talk about jurisdiction. Both you has-beens better get off my land.'

'He's here,' Easterly pronounced with unnerving certainty. His eyes never left those of the rancher as he continued, 'I'm right, ain't I, Winslow?'

Tippet never twitched a muscle, but his hands brushed the grips of the pistols that seemed a natural extension of the man.

'What are you talking about?' exploded Winslow.

'You know somethin', Joshua?' muttered Crenshaw, throwing a quick glance at his companion. 'You seen somethin' out here you want to tell me about?'

'I know why Winslow wants us off his land,' replied the old shootist. 'An' as to where they've stashed the Kid, why, that's as clear as the Texas sky.'

'You're crazy, old man!' the rancher snarled, but Easterly caught the man's quick, furtive look toward the old shed.

'I might be,' Easterly allowed, remaining calm. 'But I know you got Kid Buttercup stuck away in that shack out behind your main buildin's.' 'Fact, I'll be lookin' in there afore we leave.'

'Damn!' Winslow's nerve snapped as his hand dropped to the gun holstered at his right hip. He was pulling the .45 clear of leather even as Crenshaw's fingers wrapped firmly about his own pistol's grip.

Jay Tippet was way ahead of his boss. The gunman's pistols were out of their holsters and levelled upon the silver-haired storekeeper before Winslow touched his own weapon, and Tippet was fast.

For all that, however, Joshua Easterly was faster still. His old modified Colt Navy .36 boomed twice and two holes spurted crimson from the gunfighter's shallow chest. In disbelief, Tippet dropped his pistols and tried to cover the leaking holes with his hands. A curse came to his lips, but only a soft gurgle accompanied by a flow of bright scarlet emerged from his open mouth. Jay Tippet fell dead on the hard-packed earth of the ranch-yard while Carl Winslow pulled the trigger of his Colt .45 and shot Marshal Crenshaw from his saddle.

As the lawman struck the ground with a heavy thud and a loud grunt of pain, Easterly yelled, *'Jack!'*

In rage, he pulled trigger for a third time at the retreating figure of the rancher. It was a hasty shot that missed the mark, but at least it forced Winslow to curtail his attack on the lawman. While the rancher sought cover behind a nearby water trough, the old shootist leapt from the saddle to check on his friend.

With a wave of his hand, the starpacker motioned him away. 'I'm OK, dammit!' the marshal growled. 'Just a crease along my ribs. You better look out yonder toward the bunkhouse while I keep Winslow busy.'

With that, Crenshaw blasted a hole in the long, low water trough so that the Box CW owner quickly ducked low.

Easterly turned his head to see half a dozen hardcase ranch-hands cross the yard from their quarters at a run. Crenshaw and Easterly were caught in the open, a tough spot to be in – but both men had seen such times before and lived to tell of it.

'Let's make for the house, Jack,' called Easterly as the two men gave their horses a swat to send them clear of danger. *'Come on.'*

The duo pounded up to the porch and fairly threw themselves into the ranch-house. A moment later gun barrels shattered window and Easterly and Crenshaw began firing from the relative safety of the house while the hands scrambled for cover before them.

Winslow's angry voice carried over the sounds of exploding cartridges. 'Get them! I want them dead!'

Inside the shed, Kid Buttercup had not missed his opportunity. After a quick glance at the still form of their captive, the two guards had risen from their seats to stare cautiously out the windows. With speed and silence – two attributes not immediately apparent in the big man – the Kid slipped his hands free from the loosened bonds and untied the ropes about his booted ankles. He was free now, and moving with cat-like stealth toward the men standing to either side of the shack's warped plank door.

'Hey, boys!'

Kid Buttercup's big right fist exploded in the face of the squat, powerful Chet. The deputy felt the satisfying crunch of the nose as blood dripped freely from the smashed face. With a scream of rage and pain, Chet slammed back against the wall as Sandy moved forward with a roundhouse right that smacked against the Kid's ear with a painful whack. Buttercup's booted toe lashed out to land with force and accuracy between the other man's legs. Sandy let out a high-pitched howl as he fell to his knees, and the deputy unleashed a left uppercut that snapped the youngster's head back and sent him sprawling on his back.

As the big man turned to check on Chet, Chet's right fist jarred against his head and opened a cut along his cheekbone. A right and left of his own staggered the solidly-built man so that he again crashed against the wall behind him. Quickly, Buttercup whirled in time to see Sandy levelling a pistol on his mid-section. The Kid leapt for his own weapon that lay beside the shack's door as the youngster's revolver spat flame and thunder. A split second later the deputy filled the little room with more gun-thunder and the top of Sandy's head turned into a crimson and grey nightmare. Within a heartbeat, the Kid turned his weapon on to Chet, who was pulling his own .45 from leather. Without hesitation, Buttercup pulled the trigger twice, and send the chunky out- law to join his partner in death. Chet sat down heavily on the dirt floor with his back to the wall and let his pistol slip from his nerveless fingers.

'An' that,' the Kid stated matter-of-factly, 'takes care of *that.*'

He scrambled to his feet, then strapped the gunbelt about his hips before reloading the big revolver with deliberate speed. A quick glance at what was left of Chet and Sandy brought only a grim epitaph from the giant who now stood alone in the small, shabby room. 'You should've known better, boys.'

Almost immediately, however, his mood lightened. 'Well,' he told himself with a grin that split his battered features, 'things is lookin' up, anyhow. Whatever's goin' outside was made to order for this here ol' boy, an' I'm figgerin' it's time to join the party.'

With the Remington .44 in hand, Kid Buttercup smashed the sagging door from its hinges with one booted foot. He immediately leapt through the doorway in a head-first dive, rolled briefly, then ran in a crouch for the now deserted bunkhouse. Bullets punched holes through the air around him, but not one touched the big man as he ran for cover. As he hustled for safety, the scene before him brought an even bigger smile to a face caked with dried blood.

Crenshaw and Easterly were disappearing through the front door of the ranch-house while half a dozen gun-heavy hardcases blurred across the yard. In front of the house, crouched behind a leaking water trough, Carl Winslow was shouting orders for his men to kill the two who had attained the relative safety of the house. He punctuated his orders by popping off shots of his own that smacked harmlessly into the solid front door. Confusion reigned momentarily as the men were uncertain what direction demanded their most immediate attention.

Not only was lead buzzing toward the ranch-house – it was also flying in the direction of the running deputy, but no one was hit in the hasty exchange. Winslow's voice called sharply so that some order was restored just as the Kid disappeared inside the bunk-house. Surveying the scene from a window, Buttercup focused his attention on the rancher who was now shouting to his men in a more commanding tone.

'Settle down, boys, keep it steady!' he yelled. 'We've got 'em pinned down inside and we can expect the rest of the men to come in off the range as soon as they hear all this shooting! Let's take it easy, pick our shots, and keep these jaspers just where we want 'em!'

With a grin, Buttercup promptly drew a bead and shot the hat from atop Winslow's head. The rancher dropped to his knees and shuffled rapidly behind the water trough while the Box CW hands scrambled to sparse cover behind water barrels and stalled wagons.

'Hey, Jack! Joshua! You two ready to clean up all the trail-trash scattered about this here ranchyard?'

'Ready when you are, Kid!' Easterly shouted back from the house. 'We was waitin' on you! Don't reckon it'll take too long to wrap this thing up!'

'Let's show these boys how it's done, then!'

As Buttercup finished the sentence, his .44 exploded and a man yelped as he jerked his exposed leg back behind the barrel. Pistols boomed from the ranch-house while the Box CW hands returned fire from their positions of concealment.

Just moments before, Winslow and his men had seemed to possess the upper hand. Now, the half-dozen men and their leader were caught in a deadly cross-fire from the ranch headquarters and the bunkhouse. What had begun as a potentially victorious siege suddenly promised to be a deadly fight for the Box CW crew.

'Don't let 'em bluff you, boys!' cried

Winslow, proving that he had not become the leader of the hardcase outfit without some grit and sand. He blasted a careful shot toward one of the ranch-house windows and was rewarded by a grunt of pain. 'We can still pull this thing off! Pick your shots and keep those guns busy!'

Gunfire erupted in sporadic bursts as those behind the walls exchanged shots with the outlaw gang scattered across the ranchyard. The smell of burnt powder hung with the haze of gunsmoke in the air while an occasional scream or groan made clear that a lead slug had found is mark. Within minutes, four of the Box CW cow hands lay dead or seriously wounded and, fairly shortly after that, the roaring thunder of sixguns diminished.

Buttercup looked out the window as he reloaded the .44 with an efficient speed borne of much practice. 'Damn!' he exclaimed beneath his breath. Then, raising his voice, he shouted to Easterly and Crenshaw, 'They're gettin' away!'

But Carl Winslow and the two men closest to him were already hurrying around the corner of the ranch house, firing shots to cover their retreat. The fusillade forced the Kid, Crenshaw and Easterly to remain in their own positions of safety while the outlaw boss and his men quickly saddled horses from the corral, then sped off in the direction of town.

As the outlaw trio disappeared in a cloud of dust, Easterly shouted from his window, 'Rest of you men better call it quits!'

A pistol boomed and the lead smacked into the window-frame beside the old shootist's head. Buttercup's answering shot shattered the gun-arm of the wounded outlaw who had triggered the pistol at the storekeeper.

After a loud groan, a voice called out in desperation, 'All right! Dammitall, we're done in!'

Throw your weapons out!' called the Kid.

A few pistols clattered angrily into the yard from various positions of concealment.

Buttercup quickly stepped from the bunk-house doorway while Easterly emerged from the ranch-house, supporting Crenshaw with his left hand.

They found two dead men and two more wounded. There was the man the deputy had shot in the leg and, most recently, the arm, and a white-faced young cowboy whose breath came in shallow, painful gasps that made crimson leak from holes in his chest and belly. Easterly helped the marshal sit down on a stump in the yard.

'How you feelin', Jack?' asked the big deputy as he approached from the direction of the bunkhouse. 'You hit bad?'

'I ain't hit good, you big ox,' grumbled the lawman. He had a bloody crease along his ribcage and a hole punched through the fleshy area near his left armpit. 'Where the hell've you been, anyway?'

'These fellers grabbed me las' night,' Buttercup explained. 'It was Winslow, jus' like I figgered all along.'

'Sure, sure,' Crenshaw rasped with a long-suffering nod.

Easterly said, 'I don't mean to break up this happy reunion, but Buttercup an' me got to travel, Jack.'

'What about me?' The marshal rose to unsteady feet with fire in his eyes. 'I can ride.'

'You got to look after these prisoners,' Easterly pointed out. 'An' besides, you're too shot-up to keep pace with us an' you know it.'

'Yeah, old hoss,' said the Kid, grinning at the starpacker with obvious delight. 'Don't trouble yourself none. Me an' Joshua'll handle it.'

Within ten minutes, Crenshaw was patched up as well as they could manage. Rounding up the runaway horses was a job that required a little more time. The marshal turned his attention to the wounds of the outlaw survivors while Easterly and Buttercup climbed into their saddles.

Crenshaw looked up into the lined face of Joshua Easterly. 'You two take care. Don't let that deputy of mine do anythin' real stupid.'

'Methuselah's ghost!' exclaimed the Kid. 'I didn't know you cared, Jack.'

'You bring these boys in,' Easterly said, nodding his head toward the wounded prisoners. 'We'll take care of the rest.'

Crenshaw nodded back solemnly as his two companions left the ranchyard in pursuit of Winslow. The old lawman had no doubt that his friends would find justice in the form of a Panhandle showdown.

NINE

'Damn!'

Easterly reined in hard, and seconds later Kid Buttercup pulled up beside him in a cloud of thick, choking dust.

'What's the trouble, old hoss?' Buttercup roared, clearly unhappy with the delay. 'We're hot on the trail o' that Winslow an' his scum – ain't no need to slow down now!'

'Look there.' Easterly pointed to a muddle of prints on the hard, rocky earth before them. Numerous horses had merged on the trail at that point, and very recently.

'Methuselah's ghost!' exploded the Kid. 'It looks like eight or ten more riders has done joined up with the boys we're chasin'!'

The silver-haired shootist nodded in vigorous agreement. 'That'd be my guess. Looks like we're on the trail of a dozen or more men now.'

'That shore don't make our job no easier than it was, Joshua,' the deputy replied. He turned on his most foolish grin, then added a wink at the old gunman before continuing. 'But I'm bettin' you an' me has got what we need to get this job done proper.'

The older man simply smiled in response, then touched heels to his horse. The two men thundered off toward Spit Junction without further dialogue. Each man knew the odds against them, but each was equally determined to see Winslow and his crew brought to justice.

Intent on making fast time along the trail, Easterly almost missed the flash of sunlight reflecting from the rifle barrel. Almost – but not quite. Hunching forward in the saddle even as the Winchester boomed, he felt the ragged tear open across his shoulders and leak crimson to dampen his shirt. Another gun sounded from the opposite side of the dusty town road as the two men pulled up to seek cover among the large rocks that littered both sides of the trail.

'What the hell?' growled Buttercup, dismounting hurriedly and scrambling behind a small cluster of brush and rocks along one side of the road. 'Them outlaws is considerably smarter than I done give 'em credit fer!'

'That's a fact,' Easterly agreed from his own location on the opposite side of the open, dusty trail. 'Let's see what we're up against.'

He popped off a shot at each of the high rocks behind which the gunmen were concealed, with the desired response. Rifles boomed and lead screamed as it ricocheted among the scattered rocks.

'There's just two of 'em.'

'Two's enough, if they can keep us pinned down here!' the Kid grumbled with feeling. 'Say, you OK, partner?'

'I got a nasty crease across my shoulders, but I'm still in the game, Kid.'

Buttercup snapped off a couple of shots, but was forced to keep low as the rifles opened a deadly fire on their scanty defences. Rock fragments and gritty dirt sprayed about his head and the big man cursed in loud tones as he pawed grit from his eyes.

'If we stay here much longer, we'll lose Winslow fer shore,' the Kid complained.

'I believe that's the general idea,' came the dry response from across the road. 'We've either got to lie low an' wait, or push 'em hard an' see if they'll make a mistake.'

'I ain't never waited on nothin'!' yelled Buttercup. And even as he spoke, he was on his feet with the big .44 spitting lead toward the bushwhacker on his side of the road. Easterly was close behind, following the same strategy as he rushed the gunman's position in the small pile of boulders just ahead.

Weapons boomed and thundered along the desolate Panhandle road, and Buttercup quickly found a target for his smoking Remington. The deputy's two previous shots had blasted rock fragments into his adversary's face, causing the man to stand erect for a brief moment in order to escape the sharp stone tormentors. Two more shots from the Kid's pistol and scarlet stains suddenly blossomed on the owlhoot's chest before he slumped forward over the boulder that had so recently provided concealment. The man then slid into a heap at the foot of the rocky outcropping from which he had first ambushed the two riders.

Easterly, by contrast, was not so lucky. His .36 boomed twice with a similar result, except that when bushwhacker number two rose from his stone defence, he placed a lucky shot that chewed a shallow furrow along the meaty portion of the hardware store man's left arm. It was Kid Buttercup who brought the man down, with two more deadly blasts from the Remington. Caught high in the chest and throat, the second bushwhacker tumbled backward with a high-pitched scream of pain. After that, silence descended over the bloody battle-site. All was stillness for a brief moment, as the two survivors quickly reloaded their weapons.

Finally shoving his pistol into its holster, the old shootist faced his shaggy companion and met his steady gaze. 'Thanks,' he said quietly.

'No need fer it,' the Kid replied with a wide grin that showed off some of the gaps where his teeth were missing. 'It took both of us to do the job right. If you hadn't flushed the mangy coyote out, then I shore couldn't've shot him down.'

'I ain't as fast as I used to be,' Easterly observed with a solemn shake of his head. 'Fact, I've slowed considerable.'

'No reason for a hardware store man to be fast with a gun, now, is there, Joshua?' Buttercup asked with a smile and a wink. 'Right – we'd best get you patched up so's we can get movin' again.'

'That'll take time,' growled his companion. 'An' time's the one thing we ain't got.'

'It won't help nothin' iffen you're too weak to pull a trigger,' Buttercup pointed out as he made quick work of cleaning and dressing his companion's two ragged, bloody wounds.

Minutes later, the task completed, the Kid moved toward his horse while calling over his shoulder, 'You gonna take your ease or git movin' fer town, old man?'

'I'm right with you, Kid!'

Easterly scrambled to his feet, but swayed a bit as he stomped off toward his horse.

The two men were mounted and pounding in the direction of town within the space of heartbeats. The entire episode had cost them only fifteen minutes, but it was a quarter-hour they couldn't afford to waste. Already Winslow and his gang might have made good their escape.

Hating to do it, for both men were great respecters of horseflesh, they pushed their mounts hard in an effort to close the gap, and by the time they pulled up before the Emerald Palace, both horses were lathered and weaving.

Gerry O'Cooners was pushing through the doorway as Buttercup and Easterly slid down off their saddles. The big barkeep shouted his query through the dust and noise of their arrival. 'Mither of God! What's all the commotion?'

'Did Winslow and his boys just come through here?' Easterly barked urgently.

'Sure they did,' the Irishman responded. 'They jus' rampaged through the streets not five minutes ago. An' what do ye think of it, Joshua? The whole lot of 'em pulled up outside of Miss Martha's house right now.'

The light of recognition illuminated the old shootist's sky-blue eyes as he turned and stalked off in the direction of the school-teacher's home. Kid Buttercup was close behind him, a puzzled expression on his battered features.

'Grab that scattergun o' yours an' come a-runnin',' the big deputy called back to O'Cooners. 'I got me a suspicion that that little gal is in some big trouble.'

Easterly and Buttercup quickly achieved the outskirts of town and found shelter behind a water-barrel across the street from the young woman's small cottage. No sooner had they reached cover, however, than a sudden fusillade rattled out to greet them. As they knelt behind their impromptu barricade, lead thunked angrily into the thick wooden slats that sheltered the two men.

'Looks like they know we're here,' Buttercup observed drily, without taking his eyes off the front of the house. 'Now what, old hoss?'

'We could use some help,' Easterly commented.

The deputy grinned at the sound of approaching boots pounding the hard Panhandle ground. 'Help's on the way, partner.'

Again shots rang out from the house, but did no damage. From the shelter of a nearby doorway just to their rear, the ex-gunman and the oversized deputy heard the unmistakable Irish brogue of Gerry O'Cooners. 'An' what will you be needin' from us?' he enquired. 'We're here, we're armed an' we're loaded fer bear.'

'Who's with you, Gerry?' asked Easterly, not taking his eyes off the house before him.

'Me competitors from the Silver Slipper've come to lend a hand.'

'Otto Wendt an' Ned Burdine?' exploded Buttercup. 'Which side o' this fracas is they *on*, anyway?'

'They're with me,' came the barkeep's reply. 'We can count on them, to be sure.'

Otto Wendt gave a simple nod, but otherwise remained silent as he stood close by with a shotgun in his tight, big-handed grip. Ned Burdine offered up a grim smile and hefted his pearl-handled .32 as if he knew how to use it.

'I want you three to hurry on around the back o' that house,' instructed Easterly, thinking fast. 'No one's to come in or out of there.' He paused for a moment, then added grimly, 'And I mean *nobody*.'

'We understand, Joshua,' the Irishman replied as he and the two men from the Silver Slipper made their way toward the back of the house. A few scattered shots came from inside, but none came close to the trio who would guard the rear of the teacher's dwelling. A brief time passed before a shotgun blast informed Easterly and Buttercup that the others were in place.

'It's time,' Easterly said matter-of-factly.

'I'm ready, old hoss,' grinned the deputy.

Taking in a deep breath, the old shootist expelled it slowly through clenched teeth before calling to those inside the house, 'We got you covered from all sides! You'll never get out of town alive, so come on out with your hands up an' guns left behind!'

'You'll let us go or I'll shoot the girl!' Carl Winslow shouted back. 'I've got a gun to her head right now, and I can kill her as easy as look at her!'

'Just come out an' be quick about it!' Easterly's voice carried clear across the street to those inside, as well as the trio around back. 'We can wait, but you're just makin' it harder on yourselves!'

'Didn't you hear what I just told you, old man?' the Box CW rancher growled back angrily. 'So help me I'll *kill* her if you don't back off!'

'Damn, Joshua,' Buttercup muttered in a low rumble. 'We're gonna have to let 'em walk. We can't put the little lady in no danger.'

'They won't hurt her.'

'You don't know that.' The Kid ripped off a string of curses, but still held his voice to a low, growling whisper. 'We got no choice but to let them owlhoots get clear o' town, then follow 'em close behind an' push fer another showdown – one that'll finish 'em fer good.'

'We'll have it out right here,' Easterly insisted, his voice cold and without any kind of emotion. 'We ain't got to look for another chance. This is *it*.'

'Please!' the plaintive cry of a woman suddenly came from inside the house. 'Help me!'

'That's Martha!' exclaimed Buttercup in a voice that evidenced his growing concern for the teacher's safety. 'They got her, Joshua, an' there ain't nothin' we can do now but let 'em go!'

'*Please!*' Martha Dorsett called out again.

'Don't let them hurt me! They'll kill me if you don't do as they say! Please, let them go!'

Buttercup gripped his companion's arm in his big, soiled hand. 'You'll have to–' he began.

'I don't have to do anything,' Easterly replied as he shook the big man's hand loose from his arm in an impatient gesture. 'They ain't about to hurt that woman.'

'You can't be sure o' that, Joshua. Them fellers is desperate killers.'

'*I'm* sure.'

'Please, help me!' Martha began again, but was quickly interrupted by the sharp, ringing voice of Joshua Easterly, who called out from his secure position behind the water barrel.

'Give it up, Miss Dorsett! You an' Winslow come on out o' there with your hands up an' all weapons left behind! It's all over!'

Kid Buttercup's mouth fell open and he jerked his head around to stare at his companion in stunned disbelief. *'What was that you said?'*

TEN

Kid Buttercup's mouth hung open and he absently scratched an imaginary itch somewhere in the bushy tangle at the back of his head. 'What in hell's bells is you talkin' about, Joshua? Poor Miss Martha's life is in danger, an' you're talkin' in riddles! Have you slipped off your track, old hoss?'

'No,' Easterly replied. 'Miss Dorsett knows *exactly* what I'm talkin' about, an' so does Winslow.'

'Well, jist how 'bout you fillin' *me* in, partner?' Buttercup requested with barely concealed irritation. 'If Winslow's the owlhoot behind all these shenanigans, then what you hollerin' at Miss Martha for? You ain't makin' no sense a'tall, Joshua.'

'Oh, Winslow's part of it, all right,' the old shootist agreed. 'But he ain't the one who put it all together. Our schoolmarm is the lady with all the brains.'

'*What!*' exploded Buttercup. 'You jist can't be serious, old hoss! That sweet little woman is a dagblasted *angel!* Why, me an' she is–'

Easterly interrupted the long stream of excited verbiage with a simple, 'Hold on, Kid. I'll explain it all after we've wrapped this business up an' put these scalawags away for good. Until then, just trust me.'

'Well, I never in all my born days–'

'*Trust* me, Kid.'

A shout from the house brought an abrupt end to their tense conversation. Winslow was calling for their attention.

'I'm coming out, Easterly!' the rancher bellowed from across the street. 'You better keep that gun of yours quiet and tell them other boys to do the same! I don't care what you think you know – you better believe I'll kill her!'

A tense moment later, Carl Winslow appeared in the doorway of the small cottage with his left arm wound tightly about Martha Dorsett's pretty neck. The young woman formed a shield for the rancher's body, and he had the muzzle of his pistol pressed to her temple.

'I'll put a hole through her head if anybody tries to stop me,' the rancher called to the two men sheltering across the street. 'I'm taking her with me, and my men are following us out of here! If anybody makes a move against us, she's a *dead* woman! You better think about that, old man.'

'Please do as he says,' Martha whined plaintively. 'He'll kill me if you don't.'

Easterly called out firmly, 'That's enough o' that, Miss Dorsett. I told you before. I know the score. I know you head up this gang an' that Winslow has been workin' for you all along. It's all over now.'

The young woman made a show of surprise and began an awkward defence, but Winslow talked her down. 'Enough gab!' he snarled. 'I don't care about anything except getting out of here alive and rich! I'll kill her sure as I'm standing here, and don't you doubt it! Now drop those guns or she's dead!'

After only a moment of hesitation, Easterly stood up and holstered his gun, calling in defeat, 'We can't risk it, boys. Gerry! You an' them other fellers put down your guns!'

Kid Buttercup left his gun at his feet, then rose to stand beside his companion. Easterly, meanwhile, watched in frustrated silence as O'Cooners, Wendt and Burdine dropped their guns to earth behind the house.

'Have you thought this thing through, Winslow?' the silver-haired gunman asked in an effort to stall for time – time to look for any edge he could find.

'I've thought it through real fine, old-timer,' replied the rancher. 'I've even thought about how to get rid of you!'

At this prompt, Martha Dorsett quickly stepped from the rancher's grasp to bring up a small revolver previously concealed in the folds of her shawl. Meanwhile, Winslow levelled the .45 on Easterly, and his finger tightened on the trigger.

His first shot went wild, which was a shame for Winslow because he never got the opportunity for a second. All at once, Easterly's navy .36 was back in his fist and spitting thunder. Two slugs smacked heavily into the rancher's broad chest and the man tumbled back through the open doorway just as his men were attempting to push through into the street.

In the meantime, Martha Dorsett's .32 was focusing on the rapidly moving figure of Kid Buttercup. The deputy quickly bent low to scoop up his pistol and in one fluid motion managed a precise shot to the little lady's gunhand. The schoolteacher cried out in pain and dropped the weapon to the ground.

By this time the trio around back had recovered their weapons, so that as the remainder of the outlaw gang poured from the doorway, they were met with a withering fire that brought their escape to an abrupt and deadly end. In the brief, violent gun-fight that followed, the five men outside the dwelling cut them down with deadly accuracy. With three dead and one wounded, the final two survivors suddenly lost their appetite for gunplay and stuck their hands up in surrender.

At last, the excitement in Spit Junction was all over.

They all assembled at the Emerald Palace Saloon in the early evening hours. Scattered patrons sipped from mugs of beer in the haze of grey smoke that hung about the faded green interior. O'Cooners served a round of beer on the house for the group assembled at the small back-corner table. Easterly and Crenshaw had both been patched up by the local sawbones during the late afternoon, and Kid Buttercup and Gerry O'Cooners had seen to the prisoners. The little jail was full, since Martha Dorsett took a cell to herself.

The dust had settled. Now it was time for

questions – and the old shootist thought he had all the answers.

'I don't get the whole blamed thang,' grumbled the Kid. 'Jist how do you figger this mess?'

'Well, it really ain't all that difficult,' Easterly began. 'Once the pieces started comin' together, I could see the whole picture.'

'How did you come to place Miss Martha as the one behind this gang of owlhoots?' Crenshaw queried.

'Just a good guess is all,' Easterly replied with a modest shrug. 'You see, I'd noticed her talkin' with Winslow a time or two, but never saw 'em together at the socials or the café or such as that. 'Sides which, Winslow just never struck me as havin' enough sense to hold up his *pants,* much less rob a bank. If he *was* involved, he had to have a boss, jus' like all the others. When the evidence began to point to the Box CW, I started lookin' for the brains behind Winslow's brawn – an' it turned out to be Miss Martha.'

'But that don't really tell us what tipped

you to Winslow to begin with,' blurted out Buttercup. 'I mean, how'd you know he an' Tippet was the outlaws we was lookin' fer in all this foolishness?'

'I didn't know *anythin*', Kid,' Easterly confessed. He grinned, then sipped from the mug he lifted to his lips. 'I was just makin' good guesses, same as you. Remember, you were suspicious of Winslow too. He had too many men, not enough cattle, an' they all had far too much ready cash on 'em to suit me. The fact that you'd told the lady where you were headed before you were ambushed along the trail, an' that you were at Miss Martha's house the night before you turned up missin', was the icin' on the cake. That got me thinkin' 'bout Miss Martha, an' when all this trouble really started around here.'

'Hell,' muttered Crenshaw. 'Even though we found loot from a variety of hold-ups throughout the surroundin' territories *and* our own local bank there in the woman's house, we still ain't wrapped this up. We ain't solved the riddle o' poor ol' Mr Philbertt yet.'

'That's a puzzler for sure,' O'Cooners chimed in. 'Sure an' now, jist why and how was the auld gentleman locked away in his bank vault dressed like a woman?'

Easterly smiled again as he replaced the half-empty mug on the scarred table before him. 'That one's really pretty easy, too, iffen you think on it.'

Crenshaw exploded, *'Easy!'*

'Easy as ridin' a longhorn steer,' joked Buttercup sourly.

O'Cooners just looked on in interested silence as he waited for the hardware store man to explain himself.

'Now, I could be wrong, but here's the way I see it,' the old shootist said in a slow, deliberate tone. 'It was a couple of the Box CW boys who pulled off the bank robbery.'

'But that don't explain nothin' about how–' interrupted Kid Buttercup.

Easterly raised a hand to silence him. 'As I said,' he continued, 'it was two of the Box

CW crew who robbed the bank. They went to old man Philbertt's house, got hold o' that extra key from his desk drawer, then dressed him up like a woman so's they could get him down the dark street without nobody askin' any questions. Folks jus' saw a couple of drunk cowboys an' a woman, so's they didn't think any more about it. That's why the old man's key was still in his pocket, why he dressed like a woman, an' how come the bank to be locked up tight as a drum from the outside.'

'Methuselah's ghost!' exclaimed Buttercup.

'I'm a monkey's uncle,' growled Crenshaw with a grin as he shook his head slowly from side to side. 'It's plain as the nose on your face.'

'Sure an' that would explain this nasty business an' settle the whole affair,' O'Cooners added, going on to say, 'An' the roads are safe for me precious bride what will be arrivin' on the stage tomorrow.'

'You talkin' 'bout that she male-gorilly from the old country you'll be hitchin' up with?'

Buttercup laughed loudly at his feeble attempt at humour but O'Cooners turned crimson at the big man's insulting portrayal of his lady love.

'I'll box his ears!' screamed the barkeep. 'Why, I'll pull off both his arms an'–'

'The both of you just call a truce.' Easterly's voice was quiet, but filled with firm resolve. 'We'll settle the whole thing when that stage pulls in tomorrow.'

Kid Buttercup's face twisted with his toothiest grin, and he cut a quick glance at O'Cooners, who glared back at him with murder in his eyes.

Early next afternoon, however, the small group was gathered before the freight office as they awaited the arrival of the westbound stagecoach. Gerry O'Cooners had dressed in his finest black suit and smelled of a sweet mixture from the barber shop. With red hair plastered into place and a bunch of flowers in his hand, the barkeep waited impatiently for the arrival of the woman he intended to marry.

'Maybe she ain't comin'.' Buttercup suggested helpfully. 'She might've had 'em turn the blasted coach aroun' to git away from this plug-ugly.'

'Don't start with me…' began O'Cooners.

'Leave off,' Jack Crenshaw demanded as he gave the Kid a sharp nudge with his elbow. 'This ain't the time nor the place for your crazy sense o' humour.'

'Here she comes,' announced Easterly as he pointed out a dust-cloud that hung along the distant horizon. 'You'll have your lady here beside you in a matter of minutes now, Gerry.'

Kid Buttercup opened his mouth to comment, but all three of his companions offered up such savage scowls that, for once, the big drifter simply remained silent.

Soon the big coach rumbled into the small collection of buildings that made up Spit Junction. It rattled along Main Street, then clattered to a dusty stop in front of the freight office.

'Here she comes,' whispered Kid Buttercup with the beginnings of another smirk creeping into his face. 'A real live gorilly...'

His observation brought him another elbow in the ribs from the lawman at his side.

As the coach door was opened, the shotgun guard held out his hand to help the passengers step down from the interior. Easterly and Crenshaw looked on with joy as Buttercup paled, spluttered and choked at the sight that met his eyes.

'She's here,' was all O'Cooners could manage as he beheld the vision emerging from the shabby old stage.

And indeed, she *was*. Millicent was loveliness personified. Soft blonde hair framed the fair, freckled features of a pleasant, beautiful face. She was small-framed but well-proportioned, and dressed in a dusty travelling suit that complimented her somewhat busty figure well.

Without another word, the Irish couple warmly embraced before walking off down the street towards the Emerald Palace arm-in-arm. Buttercup scratched underneath one arm before letting out a low whistle.

'That there is one o' the finest-lookin' little ladies I think I ever seen,' he mumbled.

'Indeed,' Crenshaw agreed.

'We'll give them two a little while together afore we drop by an' pay our respects,' suggested Easterly.

Suddenly Kid Buttercup's eyes lit up and he turned on his companions as he un-pinned the deputy star from his shirtfront.

'I guess this makes us jist about even, huh, Jack?' he asked as he passed the star to the lawman. 'I mean, I'm free to push along now, ain't I?'

'You settled up with Burdine?' asked the starpacker.

'Yeah.' Buttercup looked a bit sheepish. 'I was wrong about him. He's an OK feller after all. You know that night he come out there in the alley when I was chasin' that ambusher? It was Winslow who put him up to it. Anyway, after that big shootout yester-day, Burdine told me to forget the whole damn' thang.'

'Well then, I suppose you're free to loaf an' drift again, you ol' saddle-bum,' Crenshaw decided, smiling at the mixture of joy and relief he saw in the bigger man's eyes.

'You sure you don't want to stick around these parts an' maybe settle down?' queried Easterly.

'Hell, no!' exclaimed the Kid. 'I ain't got a settled bone in my body. I already done been here longer than I wanna be, an' I know dear Petunia is ready to hit the trail again!'

'So, you pullin' out again in the mornin'?' asked Easterly, adding, 'I'd like to buy you a drink before you leave town.'

'Yep, I'll be leavin' afore first light, an' that's a fact. But I'll be at the Emerald Palace this evenin', ol' hoss. You know, a drink would go fine with all the crow I got to eat from O'Cooners.' Buttercup guffawed loudly, then slapped Easterly heartily on the back. He turned to the lawman with a twinkle in his eyes. 'Now, how's little Miss

Martha gettin' along, Jack?'

'She's doin' just fine, Kid,' Crenshaw replied with a slightly puzzled expression. 'Your shot just grazed her hand a bit. She'll be fine – leastways, fine until they put her in prison for the next twenty years or so. That was good shootin', Buttercup. I'd have thought you'd have been shootin' to kill.'

'Hell, no, Jack!' Kid Buttercup answered with a wink, and his infectious grin seemed to swallow his lived-in face. 'That there is still a mighty pretty gal, an' a bad gal is better than a *good* gal any ol' day of the week.'

Kid Buttercup laughed loudly at his humorous observation, then walked off in the direction of the Silver Slipper Saloon. Marshal Crenshaw and Joshua Easterly watched him depart while shaking their heads in good-humoured disbelief.

There was and would only ever be one Kid Buttercup ... and both of them were profoundly thankful for that.